T0208324

BROTHERS

BEYOND

BOUNDARIES

ENRIQUE R. RODRIGUEZ

authorHOUSE®

AuthorHouse™
1663 Liberty Drive
Bloomington, IN 47403
www.authorhouse.com
Phone: 833-262-8899

This is a work of fiction. All of the characters, names, incidents, organizations, and dialogue
in this novel are either the products of the author's imagination or are used fictitiously.

Published by AuthorHouse   05/03/2023

ISBN: 979-8-8230-0770-2 (sc)
ISBN: 979-8-8230-0768-9 (hc)
ISBN: 979-8-8230-0769-6 (e)

Library of Congress Control Number: 2023908353

Print information available on the last page.

Any people depicted in stock imagery provided by Getty Images are models,
and such images are being used for illustrative purposes only.
Certain stock imagery © *Getty Images.*

This book is printed on acid-free paper.

In memory of my late grandmothers, Kathy Barbree and Julia Esquivel, who inspired me with courage.

CONTENTS

Chapter 1 1

Chapter 2 7

Chapter 3 14

Chapter 4 18

Chapter 5 24

Chapter 6 30

Chapter 7 35

Chapter 8 40

Chapter 9 46

Chapter 10 54

Chapter 11 63

Chapter 12 71

Chapter 13 76

Chapter 14 83

Chapter 15 88

Chapter 16 93

Chapter 17 98

Chapter 18 107

Chapter 19 118

Chapter 20 128

Chapter 21 134

Chapter 22 142

Chapter 23 143

Chapter 24 146

CHAPTER 1

AS FAST AS HIS OLD, fragile body can maneuver, Mateo zooms to the closest ATM at the gas station down the road from his home. He withdraws as much as the machine will allow. "I hope five hundred dollars will get them there." He tells himself, dashing back to his car. He drives for a few minutes and arrives just around the corner from his daughter's house.

He observes how bad the neighborhood is as he turns the corner. There are children playing outside in the dark with no parental supervision. Shopping carts are in random locations, some knocked over in front lawns, others next to fire hydrants, and some almost in the road. Every house matches the others, rough and worn down, with a broken fence surrounding it.

Finally, he arrives and pulls into his daughter's driveway. He parks the car behind her van. When he steps out, he watches his footwork so he doesn't trip over the broken concrete debris that makes up the driveway. He walks up to the door slowly, thinking about all the consequences to the actions he's taking and all those there will be if he does nothing. He takes a deep breath, knocks on Juana's door, and grins with false enthusiasm.

Stefani, Mateo's youngest granddaughter, answers the door. She is very petite, only eight years old, and has short, straight, black hair. "Grandpa, what are you doing here so late?"

"Hi, *Mija*, where's your mother?" Mateo looks around the door.

Stefani points behind her. "In the kitchen." She opens the door the rest of the way to invite her grandfather in and, gesturing for him to follow, walks him to the kitchen. Stefani enters and announces, "Mom, Grandpa's here," and skips out of the room.

Juana turns around from the food she is making with a big smile. "Hey, Dad, what brings you over?" She leans in and gives him a hug, pulling back her thick, wavy hair past her high cheekbones.

He holds up the money he took out of the ATM and keeps up with the lie he told his wife, so as not to raise suspicion. "Your grandmother, Oración, fell. I was hoping you could go to my place to check on her. You can take the children too."

Juana's eyes widen with joy at the thought of going to Mexico. "Are you sure, Dad? It's not cheap to go to San Luis Potosi. And is Grandma okay?"

"Yes, and she is fine. I just worry about her. I said I was going to come down and check on her, but something came up, and now I'm too busy to go." Mateo lowers the money to his side.

"Well, I have to call into work and get everything ready. Luckily, our passports are still good from the last time we went to Mexico. So that will make things easier. I know Ricky won't come. He's too busy doing his street crap and acting like a thug. And you know my other son is overseas."

"Yeah, I figured Ricky wouldn't go, and I knew about Alejandro. Just take the girls." Mateo hands her the money. "Here."

Juana smiles and takes it. "Thanks, Dad. We will go ASAP." She gives him another tight hug.

"Thanks, Mija, you're doing me a huge favor. Now, when you get there, make sure you call to tell me how she is doing. For some reason, she only has people entering through the store, so park there."

"That's kind of weird, but okay." Juana pockets the money.

"Okay, I'll be going now. Don't forget to call when you're leaving." Mateo starts to walk to the door with Juana right behind him. "Oh, and make sure your visit is a surprise. She will be expecting me, but I think when she sees you and the girls, she will be even happier. She will be at home, resting from her fall."

"Okay, Dad, I'll make sure it is a surprise." Juana smiles with joy. "Kids, give your grandpa a hug good-bye!" she yells to her daughters throughout the house.

The first is Stefani as she peeps around the corner and skips with joy. Mateo kneels to her level and opens his arms, hugging her tight. "Be good."

"I will." Stefani then quickly pushes off her grandfather when her face becomes irritated by his stubble. "Eh, you should shave, Grandpa." She then skips back to her room and the book she was reading.

Mateo chuckles at Stefani's comment as Kayla walks up to him. "Ah, Kayla, you're growing too fast. You need to slow down. And look at your hair; it's so long, wavy, and dark black. You're starting to look like your grandmother when she was younger. How old are you now?"

"Thanks, Grandpa." Kayla hugs him softly with respect. "I just turned thirteen last month, in September, remember?"

"Oh, I forget sometimes." Mateo thumps his head in a silly manner.

"It's okay, Grandpa." Kayla walks back to the living room and sits next to her older sister, Brittany, who is still hesitant to move and continues to watch television. "Aren't you going to go say bye to Grandpa?"

"Brittany!" Juana yells out.

"Oh, yeah." Brittany still doesn't move. "Hi, Grandpa. Bye, Grandpa."

Juana rolls her eyes. "Brittany." She turns to her father. "You know her, so difficult and at that age—sixteen."

"Yeah, I know how big Britt is." Mateo smiles, joking aloud about her size to get a reaction.

"What you say, old guy?" Brittany yells out, still not taking her eyes off the television.

"Nothing, Mija. See you later." Mateo laughs and opens the door, preparing to leave. Juana gives him another big hug just as he steps out the door. He hugs back tighter than usual. "Okay, Mija, bye. I love you."

"Love you too, Dad." Juana releases her father, and he slowly makes his way to his car with his head down.

Mateo starts up the car and watches Juana shut the door. She appears to be full of happiness, trying to stop from jumping up and down from the excitement.

He lets out a sigh while pulling the gear shift into reverse. Driving away, he watches Juana's house become smaller and smaller in the rearview mirror. A tear falls down his face. "Bye, Mijas, I'm so sorry. I wish there was something more I could do."

★★★

Juana walks into the living room with the money behind her back and observes Brittany and Kayla enjoying television. "Guess what your grandfather gave us to do?"

Brittany rolls her eyes. "Work, great."

"Nope, try again," Juana says with a big smile.

Kayla stops watching television and looks at Brittany and her mother. "I overheard Grandpa and Mom talking. He gave Mom money so we can go to Calle Mandarina and check up on Granny Oración."

Stefani jumps out of her room and lands on her feet with excitement, looking toward Juana. "Really, Mom?"

Juana shows them the money. "Yup, we leave as soon as I tell your school and I get approval for a week off of work. So in about two days. Sorry, I know it's kind of soon. But I figured it would be a great time to truly introduce you three to your father's family and other relatives. We didn't have time before, but maybe we will now." She smiles.

Just as the excitement reaches its peak and everyone is smiling and discussing how fun their time in Mexico will be, Ricky, the oldest and shortest of Juana's two sons, opens the door. He has a buzzed head, is covered with gang tattoos from head to toe, stands five feet five inches tall, and weighs 160 pounds. He walks into the living room as the girls are discussing Mexico. "Did I hear right? Are you really thinking about going to Mexico?"

Stefani, not aware of the negative body language Ricky is sending out, responds with cheer. "Yup, can't wait. It's going to be so much fun. And I might be able to see my dad's side of the family too."

Juana looks at her son and places her hands on her hips, "I already know the answer, but I'll ask anyway. Do you want to come and maybe see your dad and other brothers and sisters?"

"Hell no! My father's garbage; forget them all. I'm fine with the family I have now." Ricky says. "And you're dumb if you think this is a good idea." Ricky looks at his mother as if she is insane. "Please,

Mom, reconsider. It's like the Wild West over there, and people are getting decapitated and taken just because these gang members think all Americans have money."

"Ah, what do you know?" Juana says. "I'm going to bed; I have a busy day tomorrow."

"Fine. If you won't listen, maybe the girls will hear me out." Ricky turns to Brittany.

"Come to think about it, I'm getting sleepy as well." Brittany follows her mother to the back of the house, where her bedroom is located, not wanting to hear what Ricky has to say.

"Ugh." Ricky pulls out his phone. "Just look at this video." He puts his phone in Kayla's face.

"Gross, I don't know where that phone's been!" Kayla pushes it away from her face and gets off the couch. She walks to her bedroom, which she shares with Brittany.

"I like videos." Stefani walks over and tries to look at what Ricky is playing.

Ricky, unsure of letting her see, hesitates. "Well, I don't think you … What the heck. It's real life, so here, watch." Ricky hands the phone to Stefani.

She turns the phone sideways to make the video full screen. "What's up with only the music playing?" Stefani asks her brother. "You can't hear what anyone is saying."

Ricky looks down at his sister to make sure that all of her concentration is focused on the video. "Well, they play music instead of silence for suspense; you don't need to hear what anyone is saying because it's about their actions, not their words. It's two Americans, a guy and a girl, who got taken on their vacation." Ricky points to the screen to lead Stefani's eyes. "This man in the ski mask holding the machete is telling the viewer that their ransom has already been paid but he doesn't care. He's about to cut off their heads."

"Oh, disgusting!" Stefani storms off, dropping the phone on the floor. "I'm going to bed. Good night, weird brother."

Ricky Bends over to pick up his phone. "This is real life!" he says as Stefani leaves. He then says under his breath, "Fine. If no one will listen, maybe my brother will. And maybe he will get me some guns this time." Ricky walks over to a cabinet, opens up a door, and takes out a few pieces of paper and a pen. He proceeds to the couch, turns off the television, and begins to write a letter.

CHAPTER 2

A HISPANIC CORPORAL OF THE US Marine Forces Special Operations Command named Alex Hernandez sits in a bed at a Marine Corps base located on the east coast of South Korea known as Camp Mujuk. He is eager to open a package full of letters, knowing it is from his family. This is his third year away from home. A potential terrorist group that has separated from the North Korean regime is rumored to have as its main prerogative an attack on the United States. Although the United States cannot react until the certainty is higher, reconnaissance will be needed. This sensitive task is specific to Alex and the team he is a part of; therefore time home is not an option anytime soon.

He slits the package open with his KA-BAR knife and drops all the letters next to him. He organizes the dates they were delivered. As he is overseas, mail does not get delivered to him a letter at a time. He starts to read each one, from the earliest date to the latest.

Alex feels elated when he comes to a letter from his girlfriend, but his happiness departs when he sees it is a Dear John letter telling him good-bye. He makes a paper ball out of it and tosses it into the trash as if he is shooting a basketball. This is not the first time this has happened to him and probably will not be the last. He puts on a smile once more and begins to read more letters from his family.

He finally opens a recent letter from his mother telling him that she is going to San Luis Potosi with his three sisters to visit, show his sisters around, and introduce them to their other side. Alex is the second oldest out of five. All of his siblings have different fathers that they have not met. Relationships with men were never his mother's strong suit. She has a bad habit of dating the wrong men and, even worse, choosing the wrong men to have children with; this is one of the main reasons for none of the siblings having the same father.

He continues reading the letter, and his mother begins to tell him that she asked his older twenty-four-year-old brother to come and visit his father and meet his other siblings, but he turned her down, called her dumb for going, said his father is garbage and that it is not a good place to go, especially for Americans. His mother goes on, calling his brother a jerk that will never change and will always stick to the streets as a gangbanger. She then says that she is sorry that he is not there to come and that his father was the best man she ever had but that he died too soon from cancer. The letter ends with his mother telling him that she loves him and hopes to see him soon.

The last letter he reads is from his brother. As always, his brother is a hothead and tells him how idiotic their mother is and asks Alex to call his mother and convince her not to go. The letter goes on, asking how he is doing, stating that he should have stayed on the streets, and that he is doing well. Alex then figures out that his brother is asking him for weapons in a secret code, just as in the letters before. Alex rolls his eyes as he makes out the message: "Send any types of guns you can get; we need them to take control." Alex's decision is always the same.

The young marine finishes the letter his brother wrote and goes to his closet. He pulls out a large, damaged cardboard box. It contains sentimental mail that was previously sent to him. He places the messages he has just read in the package they came in and drops the package into the box. He then closes it and slides it back into the closet with his foot.

He walks to his desk by the only window in his room, turning on the table lamp; opens a side door and gets a few blank pieces of paper out; and sits with a pen in his hand, pressed to his mouth. As he looks out the window into the full, bright moon, the light of which is being reflected by the palm trees blowing in the ocean wind, he remembers his family's faces. Shortly after, he begins to write back to his family one at a time.

★★★

Several thousands of miles away, the clock has just struck midnight in Flint, Michigan. Ricky and three other men sit in a parked car in the south part of town, talking and pointing to a party that is occurring in front of them. Ricky and another get out of the car and adjust their hoodies, becoming incognito. The driver maneuvers the car around the block, out of sight.

The two men walk up behind a man who is standing on the stairway to the front door who is conversing with several others. One of the two hooded men taps the man's shoulder and asks for his name.

"What the—" The man shows a distressed facial expression as he turns around slowly. "Who wants to know?"

The two hooded men respond simultaneously, "Rude Boys!" as they pull out revolvers from their oversize hoodies and begin shooting him and everyone around. After the two men see that everyone has taken cover or run away, they sprint around the block, get back in the car, and drive off nonchalantly.

Several minutes later, the police show up and question everyone. No one answers. In that neighborhood, no one is willing to be a snitch. If anyone ever does decide to say a word, there are always fatal consequences. The cops have no leads and no evidence except four dead bodies and one injured woman who has been shot in the abdomen and is being rushed away in an ambulance.

On the east side of town a few hours later, three of the Rude Boys sit around a burning candle in the center of a decaying table in a condemned house. The house has boarded-up windows and walls full of mold. They are discussing their next plan of action—gaining control of their city.

A tall, dark-skinned muscular man named Mark slams his fist on the table. "We need to lie low for a while and let the heat die down." He wipes his dreadlocks behind his head. "It was too risky this time. We have been at this too long. The pigs are bound to catch on sooner or later—or, even worse, members of the Blood Brothers will figure it is just us four and retaliate."

The plywood that covers the front doorway is removed, and one of the men who did the shooting walks in carrying a case of beer, with an open bottle in his other hand. "The guns are gone, the stolen car is up in flames, and you are dumb for talking like this." He replaces the piece of wood so as not to let any passing civilians peep inside. After the wood is set, he walks to the corner of the room, eyeing Mark with the most sinister expression. "We just need to be smart and keep making moves. The cops will never figure it out, no one will snitch, and by the time MOBB figures Rude Boys is only us four, we will have recruited more, and they will have no choice but to fear us. No one will get in our way. Especially if the biggest gang in Flint is in fear." He opens a cooler in the corner of the room and places all the beer inside it. "The next move is to take out the detective who is looking for us and his wife. After that—"

Mark stands to get into Ricky's face. "You're crazy; it's too much. After that job, all the cops in the city will want revenge."

Ben, their mutual overweight friend, stands from one of the lawn chairs surrounding the table. "Come on guys, relax." He tries to get between the two men who are arguing.

"My name is Ricky, and my whole life has been a risk," Ricky says, ignoring Ben. "So do not tell me it is too risky." Ricky points in Mark's face. "If the cops are scared, the possibilities are endless. Plus I have a plan to take out all the police that want to mess with us after the job. After we are through with my plan, Flint will be just like a third-world country."

James, the taller, thinner one of the gang, nods at the thought of controlling a whole city. "Sounds good to me."

Ben agrees as well. "Yeah, really good." He wipes the sweat from his forehead with his wrist, and some drops land on the rusted old table. "It is hot in this damn house."

"You're just fat," James teasingly replies.

Mark eyes Ricky, not trusting anything he says, and bends over to open the cooler. He carries off a beer and proceeds back over to the table while opening the bottle. He takes a swallows and sits. With the bottle in his hand, he opens his arms to invite Ricky's input. "So, tell us your plans."

Ricky walks over and places his hands over James's shoulders and looks at all three of the men. "Do not forget what we do this for—the good money. We do it to get rich and to help our poverty-stricken families." He releases James's shoulders and begins to pace back and forth. "In order for this to happen, we must take over this craphole of a city. I say we kill the detective at his house. We kill his wife as well, but no children. This is to send a message to all who try to stop us." Ricky stops and faces Mark and stares him down with distrust before looking away and chugging the rest of his beer. He wipes what is left of the beer from his mouth and burps. "After this is done, people will want to join us, and will see how easy it is to kill police officers. Pretty soon a movement will start, and all will want to be part of the Rude Boys. The police will be in fear, and the ones that are not, we will corrupt with money from all the currency we will get from the movement of narcotics. But we shouldn't get ahead of ourselves just yet. First things first. Meet me on the corner of Hanley Lane and Clark Street on Wednesday at dusk. That's where the detective lives. And be prepared. Bring a mask, gloves, and a gun if you can get one."

The three look at one another for reassurance, and all of them agree at once to Ricky's plan. They toast with beers and discuss what they will do further into the future if things go Ricky's way. A vibrating sound breaks up the conversation.

James takes out his cell phone from his pocket to look at a text he has just received. "Well, I gotta go. My baby momma is being crazy as always. You ridin' Ben?"

Ben nods, finishes his beer, and waves on James. "Yeah, James. Let's roll, skinny."

James makes a dismissive gesture, and Ricky watches the two move the plywood and leave through the front entrance. Once the two members are out of sight, Ricky turns his view to Mark, knowing he has no ride. "Do you need a ride home?"

"Yeah." Mark finishes his beer and tosses it by the cooler. "Let's go." He wipes his mouth clean with the neck of his shirt, then blows out the candle in the middle of the table.

They step outside, making sure no one sees them leave the house, and Ricky places the wood back over the doorway. Ricky looks in the distance at his run-down rust bucket. He parked a block from the house so as not to cause any attention. They walk down the road to the car, not saying a word.

On the drive to drop Mark off, Ricky stops by an empty park next to a river. "Rivers are one of my favorite places at night. They help with my mind and let me think more clearly." He parks in the closest parking space next to the river.

Mark looks around the area to see the view. "I was wondering why we were taking this way."

"Let's go down there, and I will show you why it helps so much." Ricky turns off his car and opens the door to get out of his '96 Oldsmobile. Ricky stops and drops to a knee and begins to tie his shoe.

Mark shrugs, opens the car door, and begins to walk over to the river. "You coming?"

"Go ahead; I'm tying my shoe." Ricky raises his head to flash an evil grin at Mark as he walks to the river.

"'Ight, you tie your shoe." Mark starts to walk, shaking his head, "Who ties their shoes anymore?" he says under his breath, stopping at the edge of the riverbank. He looks into the water and sees the moon's reflection. "I see why you come here to think. It's nice and open!" He puts his hands inside his coat pockets and embraces the freedom.

While Mark is facing the river, he hears Ricky's footsteps rapidly approaching from behind him. The odd movement catches Mark's attention, but before he can turn around, he feels a small, hard circle being pressed firmly against the back of his scalp. Mark hears a loud, ringing echo, his eyes roll back, and his body goes limp. He falls on the soft bank's soil.

Ricky quickly places one of the guns that were used to shoot up the party inside Mark's coat and rolls his lifeless body into the river. Ricky sprints back to his car, carrying the .22 caliber pistol he just used. He knows police will arrive any second because of the loud gunshot in the darkness of night. Ricky stomps on the gas pedal and flees the scene.

When Ricky arrives at his house, before he goes inside, he wipes the gun clean. He gets out of his car and walks down the street. He looks up and down the street to see whether anyone is watching him. Once he realizes the street is empty, he drops the gun he used to kill Mark in a sewer drain. Walking calmly, before he arrives back to his house, he hops over a vacant house fence beside his home. He walks to the house's fire barrel, which is located in what used to be a backyard. He starts a fire with a lighter he has in his pocket and strips nude to burn all the clothes he had on.

Once all the clothing has been reduced to ash, Ricky smothers the rest of the flames with dirt surrounding the barrel. He jumps over the fence to land in his yard and very carefully, so as not to wake anyone, sneaks up to his house. He slides the key into the door slowly and turns the knob ever so lightly. The door opens quietly. Ricky makes sure it closes the same way.

He makes his way to the only bathroom in the house; luckily, it's located next to the front door and won't cause too much ruckus when the shower starts up. Ricky washes his body of his sins and finds a white shirt and some gym shorts to wear in a garbage bag located next to the toilet and out of anyone's way.

Refreshed and feeling like a whole new person, Ricky makes his way to the couch and drops his body on it. He fluffs the throw pillow and covers his body with the blanket that is placed on the back side of the couch. Too uncomfortable to sleep with his night attire, he takes the T-shirt off, and tosses it on the coffee table. Very exhausted from the night, he crosses his arms and closes his eyes to fall asleep immediately.

CHAPTER 3

A FEW DAYS BEFORE RICKY murders Mark, Mateo's wife, Catalina, answers the phone mounted on the wall of her kitchen entrance, adjacent to the living room. She is a slim, elderly Hispanic woman, wearing slippers and a nightgown. "Hola, this is Catalina. ¿quién es este?"

A brief second of silence passes, then a deep voice speaks into the phone with a Spanish accent. "Mateo, put him on."

Catalina takes the phone from her ear with a rude expression. "Fine." she places the phone on her chest and yells out, "Mateo!"

"Que!" Mateo replies, looking through the window from outside at Catalina and seeing the phone is for him. He stops stapling plastic to one of the many windows on the house, prepping for the cold weather Michigan brings. He walks to the front door and enters. "Yes *vieja?*"

Catalina watches her husband as he struggles to step over the one stair that leads to the kitchen from the entrance hall. He has calloused hands from working his whole life, a slight twitch in his neck, and liver spots on his balding head. "It's for you." She hands over the corded phone. "I don't know who it is. They just asked for you."

Confused by her reaction, Mateo wonders who this might be. He respectfully removes the phone from Catalina's grasp and sets it down on the counter. He takes off his coat and hangs it on a rack. Mateo picks the phone back up and, using his shoulder, holds the phone to his ear, leaving his hands free so he can reload the stapler he was using to place the plastic on the windows. "This is Mateo," he says with a warm, comfortable voice, watching Catalina walk back to her wooden rocking chair and pick up her tools to start crocheting again.

"It's been years, Mateo; you're a hard man to find," the voice says.

Still Mateo is confused about who this might be. "Who is this?" Mateo knows he has heard this voice somewhere, but he cannot pinpoint where.

The speaker ignores Mateo's question. "Around fifty years since the last time we spoke. As time passed, I managed to increase my rank. As my rank increased, so did our business. Now I am the leader, and I can do what I please, and with *mucho feria*, I can do what I want—like visit our old locations we once were run from and take them back over."

"I don't understand," Mateo replies. "What are you talking about?"

"Well, let me clear it up for you!" The speaker starts to become aggravated and is now slightly yelling into the phone. "I was once a small-time gangbanger, collecting dinero from small businesses, helping my *Tío*, but he passed away, and now I am the king. Being a king gives me power to go anywhere I want. I wanted to go back to a place where I first worked, where I was first attacked, to take it over once again." The speaker begins to sound calmer. "Do you know what this place was called? This place was called San Luis Potosi."

"San Luis Potosi?" Mateo repeats. "That's my hometow—" Mateo starts to put it all together. "Are you Mik—?"

"Yes." The voice answers the question before Mateo can finish. "Mikhael. And you must be an old man by now, with a lot of family, just like me?"

Mateo answers hesitatingly. "Wh-what do you want?"

"When I came back to the town to start collecting on business again, I had to make stops to all my old locations I used to collect from. The *pequeño* town isn't so pequeño anymore. The town is now *grande*."

Shaken from his past, Mateo replies to Mikhael's statement. "I know; I visit every once in a while."

"It took me a few *días*, but eventually I did it. I have made all of my old locations mine again. And you would never believe that all the old people that I used to collect from still own their *empresas*. Well, I'm holding a photo up right now that caught *mi ojo*. When I entered this store and when I went back to the *dinero bóveda*, on top of the vault was this picture. And do you know what this picture is of?"

Mateo does not reply for a brief second, out of fear. "No?" he says under his voice, lying, and praying it's not what he thinks it is.

"It's an old picture of a mother, her daughter, and son, hugging *el uno al otro*. This boy was the one who almost killed me *hace mucho tiempo*. Of course, I had to ask where he is *este dia*. The old lady, once again, was as stubborn as I remembered her to be. I tried to beat it out of her." Mikhael is beginning to sound aggravated once more. "She would have died to protect your name, if not for us finding your *hermana* next door. Your sister gave your information only after a few *chingasos*. She was nothing like your mother!"

So as not to show more fear to his wife, Mateo turns his back to her and starts to whisper into the phone. "What do you want?" he begs.

"I want an even trade. I have *mi hombre* outside your home now, watching you. Any wrong move and they will kill you, but not before finding out your whole *familia* and killing them too!"

Mateo cooperates to his fullest. "Okay, okay, I'll do whatever you want."

"*Bien*. Now let me think. I always love American women. Let's say you bring me a few American women, and we will be even. I'll leave you alone, this shitty store your mom owns, and forget you tried to kill me all those years back, okay?"

Mateo thinks for a brief second about whom he could manipulate to go to Mexico. "What will you do with these women?" he asks, hoping to find out nothing bad will happen to these women so he can use anyone close.

"I don't need to tell; it's none of your business. All you need to know is that we will be even. But since you're being so cooperative, I'll most likely make them my wives, or something of the sort."

Mateo raises an eyebrow. "So they won't be harmed?"

"You have my word; now I'll give you *una semana* to bring them to me. Where should we pick them up? How about in front of your mother's *tienda*? Will that do?" Mikhael laughs. "Why am I asking? Of course it will do. Have them park at the store, and I'll have my men look for American plates five days from now. Oh, I almost forgot. If you plan on sending them earlier, call me on this number."

Mateo struggles to find a writing utensil. He searches the cabinet doors that are closest to him, also vigorously opening and closing several drawers, before finally finding a broken pencil. Unable to find any pieces of scrap paper, he writes the number Mikhael gives him on the wall. In shock, Mateo has nothing else to say, so he simply answers with "Okay."

"Now, don't let me down, or it's your whole familia that will make us even." Mikhael then hangs up.

Horrified that this dreadful man found him, Mateo slowly places the phone back. His neck twitch increases from stress as he puts the pencil back into the drawer where he found it. Slowly he picks the stapler back up and starts to mumble to himself about his situation.

Catalina notices how slowly Mateo is moving. In fear, she asks, "Who was that?"

Mateo quickly thinks and makes up a lie so as not to worry Catalina. "It was one of *mi madre* workers, and he said she fell but she will be okay."

Catalina responds confusedly, knowing that couldn't have been the real conversation he just had. "Oh … okay?" Being such a free spirit, she ignores the situation and goes back to crocheting and watching her *novela*.

Mikhael has put Mateo in a dark place. "If he is only going to make them his wives, I think I could use my daughter and my granddaughters." The situation is crucial, and if he doesn't act fast, his entire family will be murdered. With no other choice, he decides to use his only daughter and granddaughters to save his entire family.

He quickly rushes to his coat and slips one sleeve on while yelling toward his wife, "I'll be back, Catalina!" He then hustles out of the house.

Catalina mumbles under her breath, still crocheting, "Whatever. You wouldn't tell me if I asked, so I don't care."

CHAPTER 4

THE DAY AFTER HIS CRIME, Ricky is awakened by his mother, Juana. She is packing and yelling at him for coming home so late. "Don't think I didn't hear you come in. I am your mother; I hear everything. Why could you not be like your younger brother and do something with your life instead of sleeping on your mother's couch?"

Ricky sits up and rubs the sleep out of his eyes. "Are you done?"

Juana says a short Catholic prayer, looking up to the ceiling with frustration, then kisses his forehead. "The girls and I are leaving for Mexico in a few."

He shakes his head, stands, and places both of his hands together in a begging stance, following his mother around the house. "Please do not go. It will not be safe."

Ricky halts abruptly when Juana stops to swing her long, wavy black hair behind her to have a clear view of him. She tries to use her deep, dark brown eyes for convincing. "Everything will be fine, *mijo*; this is not my first time going or my last."

Ricky drops his hands. "It is different this time. I know the streets, and I know what is going down in that country. It's much worse than last time you went."

"I know how to handle myself. And like I said, I have been there before. It is not as bad as you think."

Ricky looks down, shaking his head, showing signs of frustration from Juana rolling her eyes as she walks away. His thoughts tell him she does not think of him as a streetwise gangbanger because of his short stature. At this moment, he quits following her as she walks into Brittany and Kayla's room to check on their progress.

Ricky, extremely annoyed, drags his feet back into the dining room. He picks up the television remote and pushes the red button located on the top right part of the controller to turn the television on, blocking out the voice of his mother, who is yelling at his sisters to hurry up. Before sitting back down on the couch, he grabs the white shirt that he placed on the coffee table before he went to sleep and puts it on.

He flips the television to the news. Ricky smirks at what he sees. A detective in charge of the investigation from the recent shooting Ricky was involved in is being interviewed. The agent stands behind a podium. "The shooting on Second Street was done by a former gang member and rival of the gang that was hosting a party. The gang took their revenge and killed the suspect of the shooting. He was found in the river later that night. His pistol that he used to commit the crime with was found also on his body. This is all we have for the moment. We will keep you posted." The detective steps off the stand and walks off to his police vehicle as the reporters jam microphones in his face, still insisting on asking questions, knowing he might have more information.

Ricky turns off the television and looks down, thinking with a chuckle, *They are not looking for me and the crew. That was a good idea setting up Mark. We are still under the radar.* He looks to the left and hears what sounds like someone hitting a wall with a hammer. It is two of his sisters, Kayla and Stefani. They are all packed up and ready to go. Their luggage is too heavy for them, so they are wobbling like two penguins, bouncing from wall to wall.

"Stefani, are you ready to meet your dad and his family?" Ricky asks his baby sister.

Stefani, still wobbling to the door, responds, "I have been talking to my dad and his family for a while now; I could not be more excited." She smiles from ear to ear.

Ricky tries not to laugh at how odd Stefani looks with her luggage and how it is almost the same size as her tiny body. "Well, that's good." He turns his head toward Kayla, who is slightly ahead of Stefani. "How about you, Kayla? Are you excited to finally meet your pops and his family? I heard he was nicer than Stefani's dad."

The thirteen-year-old Kayla, not looking too happy, drops her luggage and places one hand on her hip as her mother does. "I am only going to sightsee and nothing else. I don't care if I see my low-life father or not." She picks the suitcase back up and proceeds to the van outside with tiny Stefani following with a huge smile on her face.

Ricky jumps up off the couch and follows. "Then do you want to stay here with me, Kayla?"

"No, I want to see the sights, remember? I just told you." She rolls her eyes at Ricky's constant nuisances of persuasion.

Ricky runs to a broken screen door. Half the screen is ripped, giving the illusion of a flag in the wind. He holds it open for the two, who are still struggling with their bags. "Yeah, I just heard you say you didn't want to see your low-life father, and that's it." Once his two sisters pass, he lets the door close by itself and follows them. He yields for a second to gaze upon the vehicle's appearance. It's a little rusty, with the blue paint chipping away. The van has seen better days but runs like it's fresh off the dealers' lot. Ricky has no concerns when it comes to rust buckets traveling long distances.

Ricky watches his step so as not to walk in any broken glass with his bare feet. With nothing to slow him down, he passes his two younger sisters. When he arrives at the van, he notices that Brittany, the oldest of his sisters, is already in and ready to go.

"Wow, I didn't even hear you get ready. Why don't you want to stay here? You don't even know Spanish."

"To sightsee." She starts to scroll through her phone. "I read that San Luis Potosi is best known for the beautiful buildings. I didn't know that last time I went, so I'll pay more attention and probably see more detail."

"Ugh," Ricky's head rolls back in frustration. "So nothing I say will convince any of you to stay?"

"Nope." Kayla opens the van's back side door, drops her luggage on the concrete, and helps Stefani place her suitcase in the van.

Juana walks out of the house with her keys in one hand and a small suitcase in the other. "There is still one more case to get. Kayla, go and get it." She orders Kayla to open the driver's door and tosses her luggage in the back, next to Stefani's location.

"Fine." Kayla picks up her suitcase and places it in the back of the van. Again feeling like the stepchild, unhappy, she drops her shoulders and walks back inside.

Brittany grins. "Yeah, Cinderella, go and get it now!"

Juana points in Brittany's face. "Don't tease your sister."

Stefani looks out her window, fantasizing about their arrival. "I can't wait to get there." She exhales just as a dreamy boy walks past her window.

Ricky places one hand on top of the van and peeks through the side door to look at Stefani, "Well, you've got a long way since Mom doesn't want to take a flight."

Juana starts to adjust all the mirrors. "It's cheaper, plus the girls can see all the states while we drive to Mexico. It will be fun."

Ricky walks over to his mother's window, full of doubt. "If you say so."

Out of excitement, Stefani bounces up and down, holding the sides of her mother's seat, still sitting. "Yeah, the drive is goin' to be fun."

Ricky glances at Brittany, who is applying makeup using the passenger visor mirror. Brittany gives Stefani a smug look. "You were too young to remember, but last time we went to Mexico, it took forever." Their brother laughs out loud, seeing Brittany roll her eyes after she notices Juana's body language change in the most sinister manner toward her. "I mean it was *suu-per* fun," she says sarcastically for everyone to hear, hoping it pleases her mother.

"Smart ass," Ricky says, leaning into the driver's window while observing Brittany placing foundation on her face. "Do you always have to put makeup on wherever you go? You know, no one is going to see you."

Brittany stops applying makeup and gives Ricky an evil eye. "Mind your own business, Ricky." She continues with the makeup.

Their mother ignores her two children bickering as they have done since childhood and looks to the front door of the house. "Where is that girl?" Juana says under her breath. She honks the horn, gently moves Ricky aside, and pops her head out the window. "What are you doing, Kayla!" She moves her head back inside the van.

The house's screen door flies open. "It's heavy!" Kayla looks as if she is dragging a mini refrigerator.

Ricky runs to Kayla's side, thinking she is exaggerating. "It's not that heavy." He takes it away from Kayla and tries to pick it up. "Oh shit, it's heavy."

Kayla places both hands on her hips. "See, I told you."

Ricky starts to drag it. "Yeah, you're right." He struggles to put it in the van and rolls it into the rearmost seat. "What do you have in the bag, Mom? Damn."

Juana gives Ricky a frown. "Don't speak to me like that." She puckers her full lips. "If you must know, it's gifts for your sister's siblings."

Stefani claps her hands with joy. "Yeah, I can't wait to meet my two brothers and sister. Mom tells me I look just like them. I saw pictures, and I don't think so, but I'm sure it will be different when I see them in person."

Ricky smiles at Stefani's cute obliviousness. "I'm sure they are going to be happy to see you as well. What about you two." Ricky points to Brittany and Kayla, trying to brighten his persona. "Are you both as excited to see your sisters and brothers?"

"I don't have any." Brittany looks away from the conversation, continuing to look at herself in the mirror.

"Oh." Ricky pushes air toward Brittany's sassy attitude. "Whatever." He looks in Kayla's direction. "Well, how about you?"

Kayla hops inside the van and replies in her smart-alecky way, "All I've got is a baby brother; babies poop and cry, so no." she shuts the side van door and hunches her way to the rear seat to situate herself between all the luggage.

"Everyone buckle up." Juana starts the van. "Do we have everything?" She looks behind her at Kayla and Stefani.

"I think," says Kayla.

"That's good enough for me." Juana turns back around to look at Ricky.

Brittany looks at Juana. "I hate when you say that, Mom."

"Me too." Ricky turns his back to the van and leans against it while looking up to the open blue sky.

"It's okay. If we are missing something, I have enough money to buy it," said Juana.

Ricky leans away from the van and focuses his view on his mother. "But not enough for plane tickets? That's promising."

Juana places her hand on top of Ricky's hand, looks into his dark brown eyes, and pulls his ear slightly to show her motherly love. "We will be fine, son. Don't worry." She rubs his buzzed hair and slaps his cheek slightly. "Stay out of trouble while we are gone, mijo."

"As you told me, don't worry. I have never got into trouble, and I never will. I am very smart, and when you get back, everything will be different."

"I hope so." Juana smiles at the thought of Ricky finding a job, leans out the window, and hugs Ricky.

Ricky stops hugging his mother and moves away from the van. "Well, see you all soon. Love you all, and be safe." He waves them off.

Juana looks back and reverses the van, and together they shout, "Love you too! See you later!" as they drive off, waving back at Ricky.

Ricky bows his head in grief and moves a pebble he found in the broken driveway with his big toe. He looks up, and the van is out of sight. He turns to the house and frowns at the shape it's in. Its painted multiple colors and the paint is chipping away, it's full of old bullet holes from past cross fire, and shingles from the roof lie in the dead lawn.

He mumbles to himself, "Forget this house. We deserve better. I promise you girls that when you come back, I will own this city and we will have a better place." Ricky walks back inside sulking. He just can't help but have a bad feeling about his family's trip.

CHAPTER 5

THE SPEED THE VAN IS moving on the expressway makes surrounding objects whip by. Juana finds it interesting to observe Stefani in the rearview mirror trying to keep her eye on each tree as they drive along. Stefani is unable to sit still because of the excitement and the adrenaline still pumping through her veins. Curious at her daughter's behavior, she examines more intently as Stefani pushes her window out, unbuckling her seat belt to sit on her knees. She pushes her lips out the window. "Woo-hoo!" she yells out.

Juana takes her eyes off the road, glaring to the back. "Stefani! Buckle back up before you get hurt."

"Okay, Mom." At a snail's pace, Stefani situates herself to sit back down, unamused at her mother's demand. She brings the buckle across her body. "I'm just excited about Mexico. Aren't you guys?"

Brittany rolls her eyes, and Kayla mumbles under her breath, "Not to see my father; that's for sure."

"What was that, Kayla?" Juana quickly glances at Kayla in the rearmost seat through the rearview mirror.

"I said Mexico will have a lot of cool things to see." She shakes her head knowing that's not what she said but that it will keep an argument at bay. Her eyes proceed to look out the window.

"Oh, okay, that's what I thought, mouth," Juana says in an attempt to obstruct Kayla's mood. "And you're going to meet your papa, no exceptions; it will be good for you."

"No, it won't," Kayla replies, mumbling under her breath once again.

Juana, knowing Brittany doesn't want an argument to happen in such a confined space, allows Brittany to interrupt to change the mood.

"Yeah, San Luis Potosi is known for—"

"Their beautiful buildings and land structures," Stefani says, interrupting Brittany.

"I guess I can't ever finish a sentence with Ms. Known Facts around me, can I?" Brittany sarcastically speaks out.

"Nope. I guess I just know a lot," Stefani replies to Brittany, not catching the sarcasm.

Hours come and go, and the sisters bicker back and forth, as sisters will. Soon conversations fade, leaving only the sound of the radio. The day eventually becomes the late hours of night. Juana wipes the sleep from her eyes and takes a drink from her sweet creamed coffee, just picked up from a pit stop to fill up on gas and buy some small snacks to keep hunger from creeping up. With the girls sound asleep, she squints her eyes. On the horizon is the exit she needs to take. She reaches over and wiggles Brittany's leg. "Wake up; we are close to Dolores's house."

Brittany moves her seat from the reclined position to be upright. She picks away the eye discharge that accumulated during her slumber and witnesses all the lights illuminating the big city. She looks behind her and sees that Stefani is unbuckled and has moved next to her sister Kayla, drooling on top of her lap. "Hey, wake up, you two! We are coming to Dolores's house! I figured that since we will be driving through her city, we should visit—and sleep, even if it's just a few hours. I can't drive nonstop without some sleep. That's too reckless."

Kayla snaps to reality before Stefani. "Ew, disgusting, you slobbered all over me, Stefani!" She tries to wipe her lap dry.

Stefani wakes from the shove Kayla gives her to the side of her head. "Oh, sorry, I didn't mean to. You're just so comfy." She shrugs and uses the back of her hand to remove the excess saliva from her lips.

Brittany, still looking toward the two girls, sees a huge wet spot on Kayla's jeans. She covers her mouth and quietly chuckles at Kayla's misfortune and how Stefani is always so cheerful no matter what the circumstance is. The situation is too funny to ignore.

"So where are we now?" Stefani looks around. "Mexico?"

Juana pulls up in the long driveway off a busy road surrounded by several lodging businesses and the highway. She parks the van next to a nice newer-model sports car. The house is one story, is long, and has a small shed next to it in the tiny backyard. The place is well taken care of. "We are pulling up to your third cousin Dolores's house. We are still in the US, Stefani." Juana pulls the gear handle to park and turns off the van. "We are going to chitchat for a sec. I haven't seen her since the last time we went to Mexico." Juana views the beautiful residence her cousin lives in. "She has always kept up with the house maintenance … so many memories." Juana says to herself.

Kayla opens the side door and is the first to get out. She reaches for the sky and gives a well-deserved stretch. "It's so late; won't we wake them?"

"It's morning now, and I texted her not too long ago. She said it was okay; she gets up early to go to work anyways." Juana opens the door and steps out of the van.

Stefani maneuvers along the side of the baggage next to her and hops out of the van as well. She looks up and sees that the moon is full. "What city are we in? And are we close to Mexico?"

"What happened to Ms. Known Facts?" Brittany rudely asks her sister.

"I don't know." Stefani shrugs off the question and follows behind her mother and Kayla to the front door.

"Be nice to your sister, Brittany." Juana knocks on the door. "We are in Laredo, Texas, and we are fifteen minutes or so from the border."

"Oh, okay." Stefani sees an elderly woman open the door and drop some makeup brushes out of excitement.

Dolores gives Juana a hug. She has short well-groomed gray hair and thick-framed glasses; she looks to be a sharp businesswoman. "Hola, cuz." She lets go of Juana and steps back to invite the girls inside. "Por favor entra. I'm just finishing up with my makeup; I'll be out of the bathroom soon," she says, picking up the brushes she dropped. She walks down a hall to the back of the house to reenter the bathroom. "Help yourself to the fridge. Make yourself at home."

Kayla nudges Stefani and whispers, "Take your shoes off." She points to the clean white carpet and to what Brittany is doing.

With only socks on, Brittany proceeds further into the house. The carpet is so soft she can't help but ask herself, "Wow, is this memory foam carpet?"

Dolores overhears Brittany's rhetorical question from the bathroom and answers with pride. "Actually, it is."

Stefani trots to the fridge and is the only one to accept Dolores's invitation to the side-by-side refrigerator. She opens both doors. One door is for the freezer, and the other is for the refrigerator. She blocks out the burst of bright light with one hand to scan through all the food. She spots a pack of links on the many shelves in the cooler. "Yum, cold hot dogs," she says out loud before opening the package and taking one of several out. In two bites, the link is devoured. She lets out a burp and closes the doors. She then takes off to a recliner in the living room and sits down.

"What do you say, Stefani?" Juana sits on the couch between Brittany and Kayla.

Stefani reclines the chair to get comfortable. "Um … thank you, Dolores!" She rolls away from the two lights that are on in the kitchen and the hallway. She tucks her knees into her shirt to form a type of fetal position and closes her eyes.

"I think Mom was asking you to say excuse me, nasty," says Brittany, shaking her head at Stefani.

Dolores walks from around the corner, done with her makeup and smirking at the silliness of Stefani. "No one else is hungry? I have a lot more than just cold hot dogs." She smiles and looks at Stefani, who seems to be already sleeping. "Mija, I don't know how you can eat cold hot dogs." Dolores's body gives off a shiver. "Gross."

Juana stands up to interact with Dolores better. "Yeah, her diet has always been weird. The kids just ate a few hours ago—fast food. Stefani ate that wiener just because she's a weirdo." She smiled at the thought of how unique all her children are. Her view changes to look over her shoulder at Brittany and Kayla adjusting themselves to a desired comfort so falling asleep will not take as long. "So how have you been, cuz?" Juana's perspective changes as she walks around the kitchen behind her cousin, who is making her lunch.

"I've been okay; just been keeping busy ever since Dad died." Dolores gets out enchilada leftovers from the refrigerator and proceeds with placing some in a plasticware container.

"Yeah, my dad told me about Tio Benito." Juana looks away in grief. "I would have come up, but money's a little tight. I'm sorry."

"It's okay, just lonely. I wish I could have had children, but you know how God works." Dolores appears to be buoyed by her beliefs, and then she changes the subject. "So your text said you're going to Mexico to visit your grandmother because she fell? Why isn't Mateo with you? And doesn't your aunt live right next to the store for reasons like this?"

"Yeah, she does." Juana thinks for a brief second, rubbing her chin. "Come to think about it, he never gave me a legit answer why he didn't want to come; he just said he was busy with something. You're also right about Tia Maria." She starts to think more intensely about the situation.

Dolores zips up the lunch box and takes her keys from a row of hooks she has on the wall in the kitchen. "That's weird; he loves his mother too much not to come. I remember years ago, when he just left Mexico with your mama, that's all he talked about—his sister as well, of course. I guess whatever it was had to be really important."

"Yeah, I didn't ask many questions. He paid for it all, so I just agreed. I guess I was too excited to ask further into detail." Juana shrugs the thought away.

Juana listens to Dolores while she scans around so as not to forget anything as she leaves for work. "Well, I'm off. It was good to chat for the short time we did," Dolores says, walking to the door after she realizes she has everything she needs. "When you come back, you have to come by so we can talk longer." She opens the door. "The key is on the counter." She points to it. "Lock the door when you leave, and hide the key in the back, under the big rock by the shed door. It's pretty easy to spot."

"Will do, cuz. I'll be leaving soon; just going to sleep for a few hours and I'll be back at it." Juana stands behind Dolores at the front door, holding it for her as she steps out.

Dolores twirls her keys on her finger as she steps to her car. "The blankets are in the closet next to the bathroom." She opens her car door. "Ciao!" she says as she waves to Juana and enters her vehicle to drive off.

Juana shuts the front door and turns to watch her children sleep with a sense of peacefulness. Brittany and Kayla are sleeping upright and seem to be uncomfortable but too tired to care, while Stefani sleeps alone on a reclined chair. The thought of being away from the real world, even if it is only for a week or so, brings a smile.

Juana unlocks her phone to set an alarm while heading toward the closet. She opens the sliding closet doors and takes out a large stack of covers and paces back to her daughters. There she tosses each girl a blanket and makes herself a pallet. She will sleep on the floor, knowing how tired her children must be. She does not want to bother the girls.

CHAPTER 6

WHAT SEEMED TO BE MINUTES but in actuality was a few hours later, Juana's alarm shoots her up from her sleep. She nudges the girls to wake them so they can get loaded up. They reenter the van and proceed on their journey to the border. Juana makes a quick cup of coffee and steps out. The sun is full and shining brightly, giving off the illusion that their path is clear. She quickly returns the key that she borrowed from Dolores to the designated location and leaves the property.

A sign reading "Mexico Ahead" passes over them. As they drive closer, there comes into view a long, tall chain-link fence with heavily armed guards patrolling along its side.

Sitting behind Kayla, Stefani instantly springs up and down, grasping Kayla's shoulders. "We're here!" She lets go of Kayla to look out the window. "Oh, cool." She grasps Kayla again and starts to shake her. "We're at the border!"

Annoyed by the lack of sleep and unable to doze back off, she snaps at Stefani, "Don't touch me, Stefani! Ugh, I can't even." Kayla wiggles out of Stefani's small hands, slides to the window, and places her head against it. "I'm still tired, and if I remember right, getting across the border is going to take forever. Wake me up when we are done." She closes her eyes and crosses her arms for comfort and tries to nap.

Stefani shrugs. "You're lost."

"It's 'your loss' not 'you're lost,'" Brittany says, correcting Stefani's grammar.

Stefani processes the new information and is quiet for a brief second. "Oh." She replies, then she instantly changes the subject. "This place looks like a prison, but toll booths as well. So cool. And there's the river my teacher talked about." She smiles and embraces the view, moving from window to window with amazement.

Brittany shows her impatience towed Stefani's attention deficit disorder. She opens the glove compartment and pulls out all their passports to enter the country. "Here, Mom." She hands them over to Juana.

"Thanks, Brittany." Juana takes the passports and places them on her lap to prepare for the process.

In what looks to be a line to pick up fast food in a drive-through, Juana makes her way, bumper to bumper through the still heat, to the first entrance to Mexico. Several different vehicles are surrounding them. Turning back would be an impossible task.

Finally, an hour later, they make it to the first booth. A rather large man that obesity has taken control of sits in an office chair with a small fan pointed at him. The fan sounds to be broken or likely to break soon. His hair seems to be slicked back by gel, but the sweat spot visible on his shirt and tie prove otherwise. "Passports, please." He holds out his hand with a lack of enthusiasm, drained from his occupation.

Juana hands over all the passports with a smile. "Here you go."

The man scans the passports. "So is this your first time in Mexico?" After he scans the passports, he stamps the back of each booklet.

"No, I came here a few years back to visit my family."

"Oh, I see the other stamps." He raises an eyebrow. "So you have the process down?"

"Yeah." Juana nods, trying to keep the small talk to a minimum so the process is faster.

"Okay, good. Sometimes people come for the first time and I have to explain so much. What a relief." The man finishes scanning the last passports. "Okay, they all cleared. How long do you plan on staying in Mexico?"

Juana tries not to show disgust at the man's sweat dripping down his face. "A week, or maybe even less."

The man starts to type into his computer. "May I have your license or ID and your method of payment?" He pauses to oversee the screen of his computer. "You will be charged fifty American dollars."

"That's fine." Juana reaches into her purse, which is set in the center console in between her and Brittany. "Where is it now?" Juana says to herself as she digs through her purse. "Ah, found it." She hands over her license and debit card.

The man scans the license into the same computer he used the passports for and swipes her debit card. A printer placed next to the computer starts to print out a document. "Okay, everything is good. The document that I will be handing to you is proof you paid and states you are staying in Mexico under three months." He hands back all that was given to him by Juana and the document that was just printed. "Now, if you follow this lane and the signs"—he hunches over, leans out his sliding window, and points—"you will reach the check-in station, where they will run your license plate and check your car for any types of narcotics or threats. There you will also have the chance to tell whoever is behind the counter if you have any alcohol, tobacco, or food." He gives a fake smile, as he likely does to everyone who passes. "Thank you for your cooperation, and have fun in Mexico." He pushes a button installed next to his fan, and the boom barrier rises.

Moving forward inch by inch toward the check-in station, Juana senses Brittany becoming agitated with the traffic. Juana understands her emotions and allows her to vent so as not to take our her frustration on her loved ones that surround her. Brittany begins a conversation with her mother. "So what's Dolores do, anyways? She has a beautiful home, and what about the car? Wow!"

"I believe she is an accountant for some winery." Because of the heavy traffic and her not wanting to miss an opportunity to move closer, Juana doesn't take her concentration off the road. "And it is kind of silly for someone old as your grandfather to drive around a sports car like that. She has always tried to stay hip, though. It's probably to fill the void of not being able to have kids and losing every man she gets because of that reason, but I really don't know."

"Oh, I guess that makes sense," Brittany says, letting her tense shoulders relax.

Time quickly passes by, and before anyone knows it, they are at the check-in station.

Juana parks the van as soon as she spots an open parking space. "Now, I'll be back in a few minutes. There are snacks and drinks in my purse. Get out what you want." Juana leaves with her hands full of documents and her other purse dangling from her shoulder.

Two hours pass, and the girls find themselves still sitting in the parking lot. Brittany turns the van back on and cranks up the A/C. The heat wave is unbearable.

"Wow, this is taking forever. How long must mom and the Mexican government take?" Stefani complains.

"Kayla has the right idea; just go to sleep, Stefani," Brittany says, looking at Kayla in the rearview mirror.

"Yay! Mom's finally coming," Stefani yells, seeing her mother first.

Brittany looks at her younger sister Kayla with a smirk. "I don't know how you can sleep with such an obnoxious little sister."

Juana opens the door. "Okay, we are all set. Let's go." Juana starts up the van and drives off. After moving no more than twenty feet, they stop behind another line.

"Ugh, why are we stopping again?" Brittany says, leaning her head against the panel. "I thought you said we are set, Mom?"

"Yeah, I know what I said, Stefani. They have to check everyone's cars with mirrors." Juana eased off the brake pedal behind a line of vehicles to slowly move forward. A tall, thin man holding two traffic batons directed their van into an open area to be inspected, only a few feet from the open road to Mexico.

Stefani is first to spot the woman who will be doing the routine check. "Oh cool, it's like a bomb squad with selfie sticks." The woman is rather muscular and wearing military attire. She has a pistol on her waist right next to a can of mace. Stefani watches the woman circle around the van with a leashed dog in one hand and a mirror stick in the other.

A few minutes pass by, and the woman taps the hood. "Estas bien!" she shouts, alerting others that surround her and Juana that the van has cleared the inspection.

"Gracias!" Juana yells out the window as she drives off. "Next stop is our abuela's store." Juana pauses briefly in thought. "Oh, I forgot; Dad told me to call him when we left. Shoot!" Juana pulls out her phone.

"Way to go, Mom." Brittany says sarcastically. "Well, looks like all the excitement has exhausted Stefani finally; she's asleep. I'm about to do the same thing; I'm pretty tired." Brittany looks toward her mom. "I think you should sleep too. You haven't had any good amount of rest since we got on the road."

"Yeah, you're right, Brittany." Juana starts to look up her father's name in her cell phone while using her knees to keep control of the vehicle. "I will once I get off the phone with Dad."

"Okay, Mom." Brittany tilts the seat into a reclining position and rolls over to her side. "Good night, or afternoon, Mom. Love ya."

"Love you too, mija." She smiles as she pats Brittany's leg to show a sign of endearment. Juana looks in the rearview mirror to see Kayla and Stefani on top of one another once again. "I love you all."

CHAPTER 7

MATEO SITS NEXT TO HIS house phone, waiting patiently in the darkness. Eagerness has overwhelmed him and tapping his heel on his unfinished floor has become second nature. The phone rings. Mateo doesn't let it ring twice; he picks it up immediately. "Bueno?"

"Dad?"

"Mija? So where are you? Have you left yet?"

"Sorry, Dad, I forgot to call you when we left. I just entered Mexico."

"Oh, so you will be at the store in a few hours?"

"Yeah, probably."

"Have you slept at all since you've been on the road?"

"No. Well, I slept for a few hours at Dolores's house."

"Oh, you went to Dolores's house?"

"Yeah, we only talked for a few minutes; she had to go to work."

"That's good. Well, I think you should rest a little more."

"Dad, don't worry. I'm fine, and I'll be there in no time."

"… okay."

"Are you okay, Dad?"

"Yeah, it's just …"

"What?"

"Nothing, I just worry about you, Mija."

"Dad, I'm fine; trust me."

"Okay, well … be safe. I love you; you know that, right?"

"Yeah, I know. I love you too, *padre*."

"Well, I'll let you go now. It's not good to be on the phone and drive."

"Okay. Bye, Dad. Talk to you soon."
"Bye."

★★★

Mateo ends the call. He takes a second to himself and glides his hand over the engraved markings on the wall from the number he wrote down previously, the numbers having been erased. As he pulls out his wallet from his front pocket, the cool lather sends a sharp chill down his vertebrae. He tosses the wallet on the counter directly under the phone, and it lands open.

Using two of his fingers, he pinches a picture book from his wallet. Turing past several family photos, he favors a particular image. It is of his daughter at a much younger age. He turns it around and reads, "Six years old, first grade." In the sleeve this photo was in is a small scrap piece of paper with the number from the wall noted on it. He takes the phone off the hook and dials the number. One number at a time, he uses his index finger as slowly as possible, trying to postpone the most difficult decision anyone could be burdened with. With much fear in his veins, he holds the phone to his ear.

"¿Se hace?" a dark voice replies.

"*Si*, they just crossed the border. They're going to be okay, right?" Mateo doesn't hear a response, just a click and the noise of a dropped phone line. "What have I done?" Mateo drops to his knees and begins to cry. "What have I done?" He hides his face in his hands, crying more intensely.

★★★

After such a long drive, Juana and her children arrive at their destination. She parks the van in front of the store as she was told, positioned in the middle of the small and confined parking lot. She takes a deep breath in to yell and wake the girls as a surprise that they have finally made it. Before waking, her daughter's confusion hits and she lets out a deep sigh. She asks herself, "Why is there no one outside? Where is—"

Just then, two spotless all-black sport utility vehicles swoop in. One halts in front of the van and one behind her, constricting her

36

movements. The SUVs' abrupt braking causes the tires to screech. The noise wakes the girls.

The two identical SUVs are impossible to see inside, owing to the tinted windows. The rims are large, all black, and very fashionable. If they were to drive at night with no headlights, the vehicles would be impossible to spot.

"What's going on, Mom?" Stefani sits upright and grabs ahold of her mom's arm, frightened by what she sees in front of her.

"I don't know," Juana responds with panic, and she quickly places her vehicle in reverse. She looks behind her just before she presses on the gas. She sees two identical men with ski masks step out of the SUV with tactical rifles pointed at her van.

Brittany tightens her grip on the armrest. "Mom? What is this!"

Juana stomps on the gas and pins one of the men holding a rifle between the two vehicles. A cough of blood is splattered onto the back windshield of the van. Kayla looks away in disgust. With the black vehicle parked so close to the van, the acceleration was not enough to give space for escape. The backlash of the crash sends shattered glass everywhere. The back of the van and side of the SUV are badly dented.

"Mom!" Kayla yells out, looking toward her mother for reassurance.

Juana touches her forehead and feels blood coming down from the top of her head. Because of the age of their vehicle and Juana's lack of upkeep with the high maintenance an older wagon demands, the airbags don't go off, forcing Juana's head to impact the steering wheel during the crash. She tries to get her vision back, shaking off the blur.

With her vision back, she sees several more masked assailants holding tactical assault rifles coming from the front SUV, rushing the van.

Knowing the automobile has had it, she yells "Run!" to Kayla. "Everyone run!" Juana opens her door and wipes away the blood falling into her eyes with the palm of her hand. Quickly she looks back to her daughters and witnesses Brittany flee from the door and observes that the two in the back are having trouble opening the door. Juana sprints back to the rear side door of the van, ignoring the threat, and tries to help shift the door. She realizes the bent frame of the van is preventing the door from opening as she tries to wiggle the door handle. Even using all her might, the door will not open.

One of the masked men wraps one arm around Juana's waist and the other around her mouth. She is tossed on the ground and quickly is blinded with a potato sack covering her head. A blow from a rifle butt causes her to lose consciousness. Her body stops moving, and she is dragged off.

Kayla watches her mother being hauled off by her ankles toward the SUVs. Not wanting to suffer the same fate as her mother, she quickly jumps into the front part of the van and exits through the same door Brittany fled from.

Stefani follows Kayla and hustles to the door. They spot Brittany a few yards away, running, hearing her yelling at the two sisters.

By the time she places one foot out the door, Kayla falls to the ground from getting hit with a Taser. A man picks her up and places her on his shoulder. He jogs off to the front SUV.

Outside of the vehicle, Stefani backs up to the door that is jammed while observing her surroundings. Another struggle erupts in the front area of the van, and Brittany kicks a man in the groin, making him fall to the dusty ground.

"Get away from me! leave us alone!" echoes through the street from Brittany's shout. She fights them off as best as she can, kicking and biting. Brittany and Stefani make eye contact. "Run, Stefani!" Brittany shouts once again before getting tackled to the ground.

Stefani is so stunned she is unable to move. The masked men forcefully place Brittany's hands behind her back and zip-tie them together. Stefani begins to step away from the van. The store is in sight and only a few meters away. She sprints toward it. As she gets closer to the main entrance, she slows and heaves a slight sigh of relief. Once her hand touches the door, her eyes close, safety seeming to be within her grasp. A quiet click sounds, and Stefani's legs become boneless. She stumbles on to the dirt and a masked man approaches her.

The feeling of being carried resembles the feeling of a car ride, giving Stefani the illusion that she is still in the van.

Stefani shakes her head and widens her eyes as she might have done if she had woken from a horrible dream, to come to the realization of a person holding her in a fireman's carry. A masked man gets into the family's van to drive off. The SUV Juana crashed into follows behind.

Stefani is tossed into the back of the remaining SUV. The vehicle bounces from her hard landing on the cold aluminum. Dry blood spots stain the back of the vehicle. Juana and her daughters have burlap bags over their heads, their hands tied behind their backs. "Mom!" Stefani cries out. Juana's head bobs from her lying position to try to pinpoint where Stefani's voice came from. A piece of cloth has been shoved into Stefani's mouth and duct-taped in place.

The man who carried Stefani violently pushes her in her side, grasping her wrists. The noise of zip ties echo as he restrains Stefani's hands and feet. After the man confirms the restraints are tight, he hits the top of the car. "Vamonos!" He yells out. He looks down at Stefani, pulls out a bag from his side pant pocket, and forces it over her head.

Stefani's eyes are closed tightly. She breathes heavily and begins to weep.

CHAPTER 8

WEDNESDAY COMES, AND RICKY ARRIVES at the corner of Hanley Lane and Clark Street. Parked with his window down, he feels the short gusts of chilling wind that would make anyone cringe. The street lights are beginning to turn on, hovering over the empty street.

Brushing off the chill, Ricky spots James and Ben, who are already awaiting his arrival on the sidewalk a few meters away from his location. Ricky opens his door to exit his vehicle and begins to walk toward the two. When Ricky is close enough, James and Ben angrily pull out their guns and point them at Ricky's face.

"Why shouldn't we kill you right here and now?" Ben looks at James for reassurance and to check whether he is pointing his gun at Ricky as well.

Ricky puts his hands up slightly and looks down both of the pistols' barrels without flinching. "I assume you know about Mark's death." He takes a short breath. "He was a liability. He was going to snitch, and he had to go. You two know this. Ask yourself this. Why was he acting so defensive the last time you saw him at the trap? And why did he want to stop making moves so bad?"

James and Ben look at each other to acknowledge and understand Ricky's statement. They come to their senses and realize that Ricky's right. Mark was acting very suspicious. They lower their small pistols.

"It was also a perfect opportunity to get the cops off our tail. As you both know, he just recently started to roll. Before us, he was a Crip. This is what made it so perfect. It made the police think it was the Crips behind the shooting, while we made a bigger name for us Rude Boys on the street." Ricky drops his defense. "Now that I explained myself, put away your guns; this is the detective's neighborhood. We don't need any unwanted attention." Ricky analyzes James and Ben as they tuck their weapons away under their oversize clothing.

"You lucky we childhood friends," says James. "Otherwise, there wouldn't have been questions."

Ricky looks at the two and shakes his head in disbelief that his friends would point a gun at him with intentions of killing him. "Pulling a gun out in public on your homie? You two are dumbasses." Ricky grins. "Follow me." Ricky immediately forgives the two and begins to step down Hanley Lane. "I've been watching this place for a while now, and I know the detective's every move. Remember not to kill the kids, just the detective and the wife. He will be pulling up anytime now." Ricky stops a hundred yards from the house and points to it.

The house is two stories and has a huge front window through which it is easy to watch what is happening in the living room. The front yard is small, but it looks as if the backyard is twice that size. Anyone in poverty would believe the home resembles a dream house.

"That is it. Now don't act like we scoping the place out." Ricky gazes to his phone to see the time, then back at the house to witness a car pull in. "And here he comes, right on time."

Ben seems confused. "That him? He looks like he belongs behind a desk to do math or something."

The detective opens his car door to stand after shutting off the engine. He looks to be slightly malnourished, and dressed for a white-collar job interview. He has a combover and a thick set of framed glasses. A pair of highwaters top the boringly studious look.

"Yeah, he's thin like me but looks like a nerd."

Ben measures James with his eyes. "James, don't say it like that. You aren't thin. You're a skeleton."

Ricky looks at the two and lets out a laugh. "Ben, you're fat. You have no room to talk."

Ben spits on the ground, overlooking the insult as he analyzes the house. "Man, whatever, shortness. When are we going to take them out, Rick?"

Ricky ignores the slight and focuses on the task at hand. "Every Wednesday night around nine, they put the kids down early, too occupied by the moment of sex-night to lock any of the doors. That is when we make our move." Ricky studies his surroundings and the two cars they drove there in. "We need to move these cars out of sight and away from the scene. We will drive them around the corner to the gas station. That is where we will wait—but not in the parking lot. It has to be off the street so the outside camera can't see us."

"'Ight, will follow; lead the way," says James.

The three walk back to their cars. Ricky gets into his car and drives off, with the other two following in James's car. They park their cars on the side of the road by the gas station, James directly behind Ricky. Ricky shuts his car off and unbuckles himself. He opens the door and steps outside his car before the other two can. Ricky walks to James's beaten-up Pontiac. He opens the back door and gets in. "When you going to fix the passenger-side mirror? You know you can get pulled over for that."

James looks in the rearview mirror at Ricky. "When you going to mind your own business?"

"Touché," Ricky says with a laugh, knowing James has his sense of humor figured out.

"Man, I'm hungry; I'm going into the store and getting some grub." Ben rubs his protruding stomach from hunger pains. "Y'all want somethin'?"

James looks at Ben with an unsurprising smirk. "Ben, when aren't you hungry?"

Ben looks at James, full of cockiness. "When are you, Skeletor?"

James brushes off the insult. "Just bring me some chips, man. I don't care what kind."

"'Ight." Ben opens the door but stops before getting out, placing one of his feet on the concrete and keeping the other in the vehicle. He points at Ricky. "How about you, Rick?

Ricky shakes his head. "Naw, man. Just get me a sports drink of some kind."

"All right, I'll be back." Ben gets out, closes the door behind him, and begins making his way to the gas station.

"Don't run! You'll have a heart attack!" James shouts with a chuckle.

Ben turns around to yell back to the car. "Fuck you, James!"

Minutes later, after Ben has retrieved the snacks, they wait patiently. As they wait, they discuss the murder further in detail.

When nine comes, the floor of the car is full of junk food and sports drinks from multiple trips into and out of the store. Each of them took a turn, keeping the store clerk from raising an eyebrow.

They wipe down their guns once more to be sure not to have prints on their pistols when they ditch them. They exit the car and begin to walk to Hanley Lane. They pull on rubber gloves as they go. Ricky pulls out a gun and puts on a balaclava. "You two have your masks, right?" He looks over to them.

The two don't say anything. They prove their loyalty by placing their masks on. Coincidentally, the three have identical masks.

"Do everything the way I told you." They find themselves in the same place where Ricky first showed them the house. "All right, let's do this!" Ricky gets a head start and begins to run toward the home. He abruptly stops when his phone rings.

James and Ben stop jogging as well, close behind Ricky. James looks to Ben, unclear as to what to do, then to Ricky. "Why isn't your phone on silent?"

"Why do you even have your phone on you? I left mine in the car," says Ben.

Conscious of the mistake, he replies, "Fuck off, you two." Ricky takes his phone from his pocket. Before he ignores it, he realizes it's a Mexico call. He tucks his pistol into his black jeans. "Put your weapons away, and take off your masks. This might be a sec."

James tucks his pistol under his long-sleeved shirt. "So we're not doing this?"

Ben does the same and takes off his mask. "What's going on?"

"It's my mom. Family always comes first. You know this." Ricky takes his mask off and tucks it into one of his front pockets of his jeans. He swipes the answering slider and places the phone to his ear. "Hello."

"This dude's trippin'. In the middle of a fuckin' job." Ben places his hands on his hips and shakes his head at the audacity of Ricky's stunt.

James pushes air toward Ricky and looks at Ben. "Just let him be. We got all night."

An unsettled voice that sounds like that of a woman who's been crying for hours talks into the phone. "Is this Ricky? Juana's son?"

Ricky raises an eyebrow in confusion. "This is Ricky."

"This is your Tia Maria."

"Yeah, you're my grandpa's sister. What is this about?" Ricky looks to Ben and James with worry on his mind.

"They took them, and they are holding them for ransom. They say they don't care where the money comes from—the family or the United States government," Maria says with one breath.

Rick drops to sit on the curb under a streetlight and places one hand on top of his head in lack of understanding. "They took *mi madre y mis hermanas*?"

"Si, they are—"

"How much do they want?" Ricky asks, cutting her off.

"They don't say."

Ricky takes the phone away from his ear to ask, "Who was it?" into the receiver.

"Los Unos," says Maria with terror.

Ricky looks down between his knees with the phone back to his ear. "I have heard of them." Ricky takes a deep breath in. "They are notorious for holding Americans for ransom and, after getting the money, killing their hostages. No matter what we do, they will die. My mother isn't anything to the government, so our government won't care. She was about to lose her job and become on the unemployment roll. I don't have money. There is no telling what they will do with them after they realize that my mom and sisters are not worth anything to the government."

"I know." Maria begins to cry into the phone. "They're also big in the drug and woman-trafficking business."

Ricky pauses for a long time as he listens to his Tia cry. "Thank you, Tia." Ricky hangs up the phone before she can say anything else. He stands to look at Ben and James.

James lifts his chin at Ricky. "What's the problem?"

"You look like you just saw a ghost," says Ben. "What was that call all about?"

"The plan to kill the detective is off," Ricky replies. "My mom and sisters are being held hostage by those fucking Mexicans I told her not to go see. They haven't given the amount they want yet, so we still have time."

Ben shakes his head. "Oh fuck man. I remember you telling us they were goin' to Mexico, and you didn't want them to go for this exact reason."

James shows deep concern. "Was it one of your sister's family members who did this?"

"No, I don't think so. It was Los Unos."

"Oh yeah, one of the cartels. So what's the plan? You know Ben and me are always down, especially if each other's fam is in trouble."

"Yeah, we got you, bro." Ben nods in agreement with James.

Ricky starts to run back to his car. "Meet me at my house!" he yells back at James and Ben, leaving them behind.

Ricky pulls up to his house in a panic, running over the curb. James and Ben are right behind him. Ricky runs into the house while James and Ben try to keep up. Entering the house, they watch Ricky anxiously going through his mother's paperwork in the living room desk.

Ben furrows his brow. "What are you doing?"

"I know most of the government won't help, but I know a branch that won't refuse. They might not pay, but I know they will use force just like we are going to, and we are going to need the help."

James looks at the pictures hanging on walls in the house and stops at Ricky's military brother's photo. "What branch?"

"My brother." Ricky holds up a piece of paper as if he has found gold. "Found it." He begins to read the paper and stops with his finger under a phone number. "My brother gave us a phone number to call him in case of a dire family emergency. And this piece of paper is it." He takes out his cell phone and begins to dial the phone number.

CHAPTER 9

THE MOON LIGHTS UP THE night. Dew moistens the grass. Tropical trees wave from the breeze of the ocean. A MARSOC team hides in the darkness of night surrounding a North Korean military base.

A single MARSOC soldier splits from the team. He crawls to acquire a significant view of the base. He slowly maneuvers around objects along his path, as a snake would, to a grassy hillside. He makes his way to the top and reaches for his binoculars to scope the area.

He places his binoculars down and presses into a hands-free device wrapped around his ear and answers a call from HQ. "This is Corporal Hernandez," he whispers.

He hears a woman's voice. "Your brother has called the main line to get ahold of you. We told him you are on duty and we cannot patch you through. He then told us your mother has been captured by a criminal gang in Mexico. What should we tell him? We will do our best to help one of our own."

Alex looks around, trying to think fast. He recalls a time when he and his siblings were children and would go to their abusive uncle's house to be looked after as their mother enjoyed the nightlife. Eventually the three were placed in the uncle's custody for this reason.

A discrete phrase was conjured between him, his brother, and the oldest of the sisters to encourage each other to ease the hardship they had to endure. The other sisters were never introduced to this phrase, not being born yet. Eventually their mother reclaimed the three once she received the proper help and motivation. The phrase consisted of the end of their turmoil and their devotion of love to one another regardless of their acts toward each other to satisfy their uncle's abuse.

The sentence was cruel and mean; therefore, the uncle would never question the motive of the phrase. In fact, he even thought of it as catchy and used it.

"Suck it up; that is what you get. You will be a wussy for the rest of your life." Alex tells this to headquarters to be passed on to his brother.

"Corporal?" HQ asks.

Alex hesitates a little. "Just do it."

"Fine. Will do. Over."

Alex places his binoculars over his eyes once again and continues where he left off as if nothing has happened. "Corporal Hernandez, over and out." He knows that if he tells headquarters that he is on his way, they will stop him and place him in the brig for going AWOL.

★★★

Meanwhile, back in Flint, Michigan, Ricky Receives his answers. He shoots James and Ben a mean look, as if his brother Alex has just insulted him. Ricky hangs up the phone. "We are on our own." Ricky begins to walk out the door, pondering why his brother would say that. He suddenly stops as he realizes his brother had used a phrase he hadn't heard in years—a phrase that means his brother is on his side and will protect his family.

"What's up?" Ben places his hand on Ricky's shoulder to show support. "Why are you frozen?"

"Never mind, we have my brother's support." Ricky turns around to look at Ben and James. "He must have had to say it like that because the military is listening."

★★★

Hours later, somewhere in the North Pacific Ocean, Corporal Hernandez jumps off a helicopter onto an aircraft carrier and looks around with his team. He has successfully completed his reconnaissance mission. As his team walks inside the ship to get their next briefing, they talk among themselves.

Hernandez spots one who seems to be in charge of the aircrafts as they come and go. He pairs off and jogs up to the man, grasping his equipment tightly to keep it from bouncing around in the gusts the helicopter is producing. "When is the next aircraft to travel to American soil?" He shouts.

"In a couple of hours, that plane the men are unloading equipment from will leave for the USA!" The man points to it while using his other hand to keep the wind out of his eyes.

The helicopter's rotor blades stop, and Ricky lowers his voice. "What is the precise time?"

"At nine hundred. Why?"

"Never mind." Alex walks away, leaving the man with much uncertainty.

The man shakes his head and goes back to what he was doing. "Damn MARSOC, they all think they're better than everyone," he says to himself, carrying on with his duties.

Alex jogs to catch up with his teammates. They are already in the meeting room, where they are to be given a briefing of the mission. On entering, he calmly walks to one of the many empty chairs facing the front of the dull room to sit and await further instructions. The troop commander walks into the room to start the discussion of the previous and new orders.

After an hour of giving a briefing of their next mission, they are to have leisure time and enjoy the next two days on the ship. The team walk to their bunks, slowly removing their gear and discussing who is the best out of them all. Alex is mentioned to be one of the best. Alex doesn't take this into consideration but rather speed-walks past the others. The group seems confused as to why Alex has not yet started to take his equipment off, and they look at one another.

Alex hustles to the room where all the mission gear is. He picks up a huge duffel bag and starts to fill his own pack and the duffel bag. The room's door opens, and Alex stops packing to look at who just entered, one of the bags still in his hand. It's Sergeant Rojas, one of his military brothers from the team.

He shuts the door behind him. "I found it funny that HQ would call you personally during a mission and not the whole team or team leader first." He crosses his arms and leans on a pipe next to the door. "So I eavesdropped."

"Are you going to inform them?" Alex places the bag back on the table and begins to pack once again. "Are you going to try to stop me?"

His military brother looks down and grins. He grabs ahold of Alex's shoulder and turns him around. "We've had each other's back since boot. Do you really think that? It's a really fucked-up situation, and I would do the same thing you are." Rojas looks into Alex's eyes. "If you need my help, or any of us, you know we are family." He turns around and starts to walk out the door.

Alex turns back to the table, and before he begins to pack once more, he pauses for a brief second. "Thank you. I have your number. You will get a call soon."

Rojas stops with his back facing Alex. He pauses to show Alex he understands to keep it under wraps and proceeds to walk out the door.

After Alex has his bag full of different types of gear, weapons, and explosives, he creeps to the surface of the ship. Placing his training in effect, he passes everyone with ease. Without a single soul seeing, he approaches the plane with the destination of the United States. He boards the plane as any normal person would do, from the main door. He slowly walks up to the pilot.

The pilot hears the floor creak but does not turn around. "No need to say anything; I got you. Everyone on this ship understands."

Alex wonders who might have told him. He assumes the entire fleet must know but are not saying anything. *This must be the reason why it was so easy to sneak to the surface without being seen*, Alex thinks to himself. He shows a slight smile, turns around, and finds his way to the rear of the plane to hide for the remainder of the flight.

When the plane lands, the pilot runs to the back to find Alex. Before anyone can board, without saying a word, he leads Alex to several crates. They are wooden and made poorly with nails. Instructions are posted on the side of the crates on yellow stickers that state they will be unloaded into a civilian factory to proceed with manufacturing.

The pilot and Alex open one of the crates and clear out most of the metal parts that are occupying the space. They take the metal to the front of the plane so no one will see the missing parts. After the area is clear, Alex climbs in with all of his equipment, and the pilot closes the crate. He uses the nails that are still part of the lid to reseal it with a hammer.

Alex sits in solitude and listens to his surroundings. He hears the pilot walk off the plane and begin a muffled conversation with others. Soon after the conversation ends, the back door opens and the crates start to be unloaded. Alex looks through a crack in the wood to verify that they are being loaded into a semi with a forklift.

His heart races when the employees finally come to his crate. Nothing out of the normal happens besides a rough ride for Alex; he is loaded in the truck along with the other crates. The ride takes a little more than two hours.

With his ear pressed firmly against a side of the container, he listens to his surroundings. A forklift operator whistles and jokes with other employees while begging to load two crates stacked on top of each other on the forks, one of which Alex is inside of. The forklift enters the factory with a bump that jerks Alex around. He knows he has reached the crates' destination once the forklift places the cargo down and drives off. Alex begins to use his body to bump into the walls of the crate, rocking it back and forth, drawing the attention of some nearby employees. One of the many employees cautiously approaches the box. She places her ear against it and gives it a knock. Alex taps back. Out of curiosity, she makes haste over to a maintenance station to acquire a crowbar from a rack.

Alex analyzes this person approaching him to open the container he is inside of. He prepares himself for his escape. Once the worker loosens the top enough, Alex pushes on the lid with the majority of his strength and it explodes off into the air. All of the workers are in shock to witness a man whose face is painted and who is wearing a military uniform jumping out and running out of the docking area.

Alex gets to a fence that surrounds the premises and climbs it with ease. He runs out of view of the workers and stumbles upon a park. He looks around and sees a public restroom. He enters the restroom and checks all the stalls and sees no one. He then locks the door and walks to a sink to clean his face with the war paint still on, having had no time or resources to wash it off before. After drying his face with a paper towel, he digs in his duffel bag, pulls out a military-issue cell phone, and starts to dial Ricky.

"Yeah, who is this?" Alex hears.

"Your brother, fool," he replies.

"We been waiting forever; where are you?" Alex then hears Ricky say with his mouth away from the receiver, "It's my bro."

"Hold on, let me look." Alex looks around to see any clues of what city he is in. He finds an outline of the park he is in, along with many other facts relating to his location, on the wall in front of a urinal. It shows the city the park is in and the state the city is in. "I have to make this conversation quick so the military won't track me. I'm AWOL. And it seems that I am in North Carolina."

"What are you doing ther— never mind. We will meet in Laredo, Texas," Ricky tells his younger brother.

"Great city, terrible memories." Alex replies. "Since I'm closer to Texas, I should arrive there before you. I'll get a motel room on San Bernardo Avenue, the road we always stayed on when we were younger and we'd visit. We will meet there. I will call and tell you what room and motel I'm in once I arrive."

"All right, I don't know much about how Mexico is run. I will have to get some info from Grandpa. He is from the area and knows the gangs and how shit is run out there."

"Good idea, Ricky."

"I'm also bringing some of my boys," Ricky mentions.

"The more, the easier this will be," Alex responds. "All right, I'll call you soon." he hangs up and breaks the cell phone in two, taking the battery out. If the government finds Alex, they will not have any choice but to arrest him on the spot.

Alex looks to the atlas on the wall and finds the closest gas station. He unlocks the restroom door and hustles to the gas station to find an ATM he can use. He withdraws most of his money. He is going to need it for the bus he will take to Laredo, Texas. He knows that the military will know his exact location soon since he just made a withdrawal from the ATM. Once he gathers his money, he walks inside the gas station and approaches the store clerk. "Where is the closest bus station and bus stop? I have no vehicle."

A rather chubby clerk with full cheeks and red hair admires Alex. "A uniform?" She smacks her lips together while chewing gum. "Well, you're in luck. The city bus will arrive any minute now." She points to the bus stop in front of the store. "You take that to Eric Avenue and it should be right in front of you once you get off the bus." the clerk stops pointing and drops her arm by her side.

Alex adjusts his equipment to his back. "Thanks." He starts to walk outside.

"Someone part of the military should have their own vehicle. Where is yours?" she asks.

The bus shows up, giving Alex the perfect opportunity not to answer. He takes off running and boards it. Feeling full of relief he didn't have to become a victim of harassment by that cashier, he walks down the dirty bus aisle and studies how is looking at him because of his attire. He finds a seat and sits patiently until Eric Avenue, trying to avoid any eye contact. His boots stick to the floor, and the back of the seat in front of him is covered with chewed gum. He can't help but think the back of his seat is covered as well. In the front of the bus next to the bus driver, a sign reads, "Next Stop Eric Ave."

A few minutes later, the bus stops and the sign changes to "Arrive at Eric Ave." Alex gets off, and the bus moves onto its next destination. Just as the clerk said, the bus station is right in front of him.

He walks inside and looks at the displayed bus trips. There is a one-way drive to his destination. He knows he will eventually walk through a metal detector, so once again he will have to put his military expertise to use and sneak his bags onto the bus.

He walks up to a conductor behind a glass window and buys a one-way ticket to Laredo, Texas. He uses cash so as not to leave a trail. He looks at his ticket to study where he will be sitting. While studying his ticket and figuring out how much time he has left to board, he walks back outside.

Alex walks along the side of the fence where all the buses are parked and spots the bus he will ride. Searching the area, he locates all the cameras around the parked buses. He drops his duffel bag on the sidewalk, rummages through it, and pulls out what looks to be a silver pen. A green laser light shoots out while he points this at all the cameras, and the pan/tilt/zoom cameras power down.

Alex must hurry; he hasn't much time before the cameras start to work again. He jumps the fence, hurries to the bus he will ride, and places his bags out of sight on the bus. Luckily all the bus drivers are nowhere to be seen. He hides his bag in the overhead compartment of the seat he will be sitting in so as not to raise suspicion of theft when he gets off the bus.

Once finished; he hops over the fence once more and walks back into the bus station calm and collected. He walks through the metal detector and boards the bus. He finds his seat and sits. Not many are riding, so he sits by himself. He waits patiently to depart the station, looking out the window, planning future scenarios that he might fall into when he reaches Mexico.

CHAPTER 10

RICKY DRIVES TO HIS GRANDFATHER Mateo's house to question him about his mother and sisters. He and his crew pull up to see Mateo is already outside and seems angry. Ricky exits the vehicle and walks up to him. Before a word can be uttered from Ricky's mouth, his Mateo interrupts him, "I already know why you are here. I'll answer everything you need to know to get back *mi hija*."

They walk inside the house. A half hour of questions later, the house is packed with family members. They are all full of fright. Ricky asks which of them are willing to help. None speak up except the grandmother. "You're all pushovers; I'll go and mess them people up for taking my daughter and granddaughters."

Ricky glares and shakes his head at everyone except for his grandmother Catalina and his grandfather. "The only one with a backbone is the old lady?" Ricky looks at his grandmother after asking around. He bends on one knee to his grandmother's height while she is in her rocking chair. With much endearment, he speaks to his grandma. "No disrespect, but that's okay, old lady; I don't want you and Grandpa to get hurt. You two are too old for this. I got this." Ricky smiles at her.

She rocks back and forth on her rocking chair, crocheting as old women do. "Shoot, I'll still mess someone up."

Ricky is amused by his grandmother's spunk. "You're too funny, Grandma." Ricky looks at his other family members and storms off with Ben and James following. The three get in the car and drive off.

Several hours pass, and the three find themselves in Texas. While on the highway, Ricky receives a text on his cell phone giving the address where Alex is located. The message also instructs Ricky not to reply because it's not Alex's cell phone.

★★★

Hours later, there is a knock on the door of the room Alex is staying in. Alex quickly answers, knowing it's his brother.

Alex looks bummed while letting them in. "I guess none of the family wanted to help?"

Ricky walks in with James and Ben following. "Nah, they all said that the authorities will take care of it or some shit. I know they don't want to risk their lives, so I didn't tell them you are with me. Grandpa told me a lot of info though."

The brothers size each other up, smirk, and embrace each other in a hug, giving in to their emotions just a bit, holding back tears and words of affection to keep focus on the task at hand.

Alex nods at Ben and James; he already knows them. Before Alex joined the military, he also ran with the Rude Boys. At that time there was no name, they were just a group of friends committing crimes for the fun of it.

James shuts the door behind him. Alex pulls out an atlas of Mexico he stole with all types of points of interest the cartel has activities in. "This is what all I know, what the military told me about Mexico. As you know, we don't focus our attention too much on Mexico, so little is known. I'm sure Grandpa gave you more to go on though."

They all hover over the atlas of Mexico next to Alex. Alex informs them on what he knows while pointing at the map. "For starters, the Mexican cartel Los Unos was founded by a group of ex-police and military forces, so most are trained in various weapons and tactical procedures. We don't have that training. What we know is only how to bust a front door in and shoot or rob the place. They will not be too easy to infuriate. The only one out of us all that knows this is me, and we don't have time for training."

"It will be fine; kicking down doors is pretty much the same as a tactical approach. That is just a fancier name for it." James undermines Alex.

55

Alex agrees with James. "I also got all of you your own fake passports to cross over without a problem. I had time to contact a few people I knew around here who are former members of the military who handled this kind of work. Ricky told me a few people were coming with him; I figured it was you two."

"Hell yeah," Ben says as he looks at the passport, slicking back his nappy hair as if he is checking himself out in a mirror.

Ben and James exchange passports to compare them with each other. They remind Ricky and Alex of kids on Christmas or children performing show-and-tell.

Alex interrupts their amazement. "Our mom and our sisters are nobody to our government. There will be no backup except from my people, and the only thing they will do is give us the intel. The hard work will be from us. I'm also AWOL, so the government is after me. Without further ado, let's hurry up and get out of the country."

The three nod their heads, understanding the facts. Alex rolls up the atlas and places it in one of his bags. They leave the motel and hustle to get into the car that Ricky drove. Once they are all inside, Ricky proceeds to their next destination—the border.

Minutes later, they arrive. James pops his head out the passenger side window to get a better look at the long line to enter Mexico. After his gaze, he looks in the backseat at Alex. "So what are you going to do with the bag full of military shit?"

Alex breathes calmly in and out. He stops viewing the landscape to give James his attention. Alex realizes the others have the same look of interest as well. "It's Mexico, and I have enough money to bribe anyone—even the border patrol. Mexico or America, doesn't matter."

Ricky gives Alex an evil grin. "Were we … our family … ever going to see this money, Alex?"

"Don't look at me like that, Ricky. This was money for my children, if I have any. My life savings. Not that you know anything about saving."

Ricky mumbles under his breath and stops giving Alex an evil frown and looks forward to traffic.

Soon after their small dispute, they pull up to the first check-in station. Alex pulls out a stack of bills. He hands them over to Ricky to flash at the woman in charge of the boom barrier. She looks as if the heat has overwhelmed her, with her thick black hair sticking to her face as she tries to blow it away. She seems to be suffering from frustration from the heat the sun is providing.

Ricky waves a hundred-dollar bill nonchalantly out his window. When she notices the bill, it dawns on her they are willing to bribe their way through. The woman gladly receives the stack of bills and the fake passports. Her day looks to be brightened, and a smile overwhelms her. She pockets the money and stamps the back of each book. Without a word, she presses a button and the barrier rises.

Alex tells Ricky to drive past the check-in station and drive straight to the soldier checking vehicles. Once again Alex hands Ricky a stack of bills. Ricky waves the man to walk up to his window. Ricky slowly hands out the money. The soldier counts the money in his head, judging by what he can see, and quickly snatches it out of Ricky's hand. He counts it again for a second with his back toward the others checking vehicles. He hits the top of the car after he comprehends the full amount of money that was given to him, letting everyone know they have passed and are all set to go.

Alex appears delighted. "I told you all it would work. Unfortunately, money talks, especially here."

After the border, they drive as quickly as possible without raising any suspicion to check out Aunt Maria's house in San Luis Potosi. The city is one of the strongholds the cartel occupies and is where the girls were abducted. They were taken in front of Maria's house. This was told to Ricky by their grandfather.

As they arrive at their aunt's house, they tell James and Ben to stay in the car and keep a lookout for any strange activity. Ben makes his way to the driver's seat, still inside the vehicle, and James to the passenger's seat.

When the two brothers go up to the door, their aunt answers before they can knock. "Vente," she says immediately, waving her hand to tell them to hurry and come in.

Ricky and Alex walk into their aunt's house. She notices their guns under their shirts "¿Cómo se cruzaron las armas?"

Alex and Ricky look at each other and then back at their aunt. Ricky steps forward. "We don't know Spanish that much. If you are going to talk in Spanish, you have to slow down."

"*Aye dios*, how are you going to get anything done in Mexico if you can't speak the language?" Before any of the brothers can respond, Maria tells them what she said in Spanish. "How did you get your weapons across the border without any problems?"

Alex answers, "Oh. Well, all I gotta do is flash some money and we will be fine. You should know this. And the language thing—I'm sure we'll be fine. We understand enough."

"Good," Maria replies. "Well, you're going to need those guns too. Mexican gangs are so dangerous, especially *el cartel*, they are—"

"I know what they are capable of," Ricky interrupts sharply. "I've already told you. Just tell us where they are staying."

Alex pulls out the atlas of Mexico and flips to the city. He places it on a table next to them.

"They took out most of the cops, so the officers are scared of Los Unos. The gang does their business in front of everyone. They have no care because no one dares to step to them." Maria then points to a street on the map and says, "This is where they keep all their women that they take for trafficking, but they knew they were American, so they might not be there and could be someplace else."

Ricky nods and then looks at Alex. "That's a good idea—to take out most of the cops and get them scared. They can do their business freely that way."

Alex turns his head to his aunt after looking at Ricky as if he is crazy for saying such things. "Thank you, Tia." Alex rolls up the atlas.

Ricky pulls out his cell phone and switches to his GPS application. He alters the settings to global view. He zooms into the street his aunt pointed out on the atlas. "Now, Tia, tell us what building it is."

She moves the view of the street and stops to point at a building. "Este!"

Ricky and Alex tilt their heads and examine the location. Ricky places the GPS pin hovering over the building.

"Now, are you sure it was Los Unos ?" Alex raises an eyebrow.

"Si, they are the only ones that drive in all-black trucks like that."

"Okay, Tia. Let's go, Ricky" Alex makes his way out of the house with Ricky following, holding a bag of tortillas their aunt gave them in case they get hungry on their travels.

The brother's aunt holds the front door open and perceives that they are not alone. "I'll pray for the both of you to find them safely and that you two will not be harmed." She crosses herself and says a prayer.

Alex and Ricky walk to the car and get in the back. "Since you are in the driver's seat, you get to drive from now on, Ben," Ricky states.

Unamused, Ben agrees. "So now what?" He looks back from the driver's seat at the two brothers.

"Now we go to a store to meet up with an old friend of mine that is here on vacation," Alex tells Ben, speaking before anyone else. "He owes me a favor. I called him when I was waiting for you guys to come to my hotel. I know you three are good with hand-to-hand combat and close-range weapons, but I need someone who is good at range and knows how to plant explosives. Plus, another man couldn't hurt."

The Rude Boys and Alex head to the store, Alex having told his friend where to meet him. It's a few miles away from their location. When they get to the store, Alex tells Ricky to pull up next to a man who seems to have a law enforcement demeanor.

Alex rolls down his window. "Sergeant Baker—or should I call you Travis, you son of a gun—what are you doing here!" Alex sarcastically asks him.

"This better be good. I'm with my wife on our honeymoon back in Tampico. You have no idea what I had to do to convince my wife to let me come here." Travis says aggressively.

"What did you tell her?" Ricky asks, butting in.

"The truth!" Travis shouts, looking at Ricky and then back to Alex. "How you, Alex, saved my life back in Egypt and now I owe you a huge favor."

"Shut your mouth." Ricky interrupts. "For some dumb reason, my brother thought it would be a good idea to get you involved in saving my mother and sisters. Either way, I don't care if you help. We are wasting time. It's nothing placing explosives. Now are you with us or not?"

Alex tells Travis with a silly expression on his face and a laugh, undermining his brother's anger, "This is my brother I told you about."

"Yeah, I know all about him and how he's a hothead," Travis says. "Overlooking the fact that Ricky was extremely rude to me, I'll help."

He then looks at Ricky. "Although she is your mother, she is still Alex's mother, and I owe him big." Travis opens the back side door, Ricky moves over, and Travis enters the car. "So what's the plan of action?" Travis asks.

Ricky points to the atlas and shows Travis the latitude and longitude of a building their aunt showed them. "We drive around this area and see how we can enter the building that is here. We are going to scope this place out to a T."

Proceeding with their task at hand, Ben drives off. Soon after they arrive a block away, they slow down and scan the vicinity. They notice it looks like a small warehouse with only one floor. They drive around the place as many times as possible until they think it is becoming too conspicuous. They park a block away from the main entrance.

The five now know the foundation of what is around them and how they can use it to their advantage. The neighborhood consists of abandoned factories and office buildings, with a few run-down houses. The area looks like a ghost town from an old western movie.

"So who has the plan?" James looks at Alex and Ricky.

"Don't look at me; my brother is the one in MARSOC."

Alex smiles and opens a bag he took from the ship he was on to give pistols to Ben and James. Alex then pulls out pieces of a rifle with a huge scope. James and Ben seem very happy as Alex starts to put it together. "The plan is a little complex. The place is heavily guarded, and there is no possible way that we could sneak in, find my family's location and sneak back out. That leaves us with only one other solution—take them all out."

"Just how I would go about it," Ricky says, smiling at Alex.

Ben and James smirk with the thought of how fun this will be.

Travis askes Alex, "You do know that when you go through with this, you're going to be a wanted criminal in the eyes of Mexico and a mercenary in the eyes of America, don't you? You will not be able to come back to the States unless you spend a long time in the brig."

"I know," Alex replies. "Don't remind me."

Ricky looks at his brother sincerely. His brother looks back to acknowledge him. They both understand what's at stake. Ricky has a sense of increased respect toward his younger brother, and Alex comprehends this. Alex looks away and sets his mind back to the plan. "I have four C-4 charges; we will only use two. I just hope our family isn't next to any of the walls when they blow."

Ricky lets out a worried grunt. "Ugh."

"I know, bro, but it's the only way we can enter. Ricky and James!" Alex points to James as he looks back from the passenger seat. "You two will use these two silenced rifles I have." Alex starts to put together the other rifle. "Ricky will be in the front building, and I want James to be in the rear building. It should be easy to get inside these buildings, since they are closed down. But just in case"—Alex pulls out two small bolt cutters from the bag and tosses them to Ricky and James—"you two are to watch our backs on the rooftops. I know, James, that you at least got a little experience in some type of rifle shooting with Ricky and me when we were kids. I know little of Ben. This is why you get this rifle, James." James catches it when Alex tosses it to him after finally finishing putting it together.

Ben looks at Alex. "Yeah, I never shot anything but concealed-size guns, like pistols and MACs."

Alex's assumption of Ben's ignorance of rifles is proven correct. He acknowledges what Ben says and continues with the plan. "As Ricky and James take lookout, Travis, and I will plant the C-4 on the sides of the building."

"So what about me? Where do I fall?" Ben asks.

Alex takes out a small rocket launcher from his bag. "I want you to take this AT4; it's a one-time use weapon. You just point and shoot. It's to fire at the front entrance as soon as we blow up the sides of the building. After you shoot the AT4, drop it and move in. Once again, blowing up the right and left sides will be me and Travis's job. But before we get to destroying everything, I need you, Ben, to go and walk nonchalantly, hiding the AT4 and getting in position to shoot it. The distraction you make, having the front guards telling you to keep moving, will give Travis and me the perfect amount of time to plant the C-4. Once you hear the sides blow, this should distract the guards long enough for you to shoot the rocket. We three will then sweep in the building from the sides and the front holes we just created, easily taking out everyone from the surprise."

Ben nods to indicate that he understands his part. "Okay."

"James and Ricky, I want you to stay where you are at all times. Ricky, once the sides blow, take out the front guards so Ben can shoot the AT4 without any problem, then clear a path so Ben can make his way in. James, I need you to be my and Travis's six and take out any one who sees us trying to plant the C-4. It shouldn't take long. When the C-4 is planted, Travis and I will back away to blow it. This job must be done quickly and before any of the authorities come to investigate the extreme sound we will be making. If it is not … Well, I don't agree with fighting law enforcement, so we will surrender."

The three that call themselves Rude Boys cringe at Alex's remark about not harming officers of the law.

"After the explosions, we should have a twenty-five-minute window before anyone shows up, judging by the knowledge we obtained from the perimeter scan we completed with the car." Alex reaches into his bag once more and takes out a throat microphone and gives one to everyone.

James looks at his with uncertainty. "What are these?"

"Place them around your neck like this. And press the neck button when you need to speak." Alex shows Ricky, James, and Ben with a radio check. "We should all be on channel seven. We leave the car one at a time. Once in place, we have to report back. This will give the next man to leave the go-ahead. We will use the night for stealth to avoid alerting anyone to our suspicious activity. The last to leave the car will be Ben, making it obvious to the guards he is walking down the street."

The five do a final inspection of themselves not to have anything out of place. They adjust their radios once more to fit perfectly around their necks.

Alex looks toward the group with much confidence. "We all meet in this car when we are done. Don't worry about prints, and keep your guns. Are we clear on the plan?" Alex looks to all of them to see nods from the group. "We move at midnight."

James smiles. "My favorite time."

CHAPTER 11

RICKY IS THE FIRST TO leave the car. He holds on to his weapon tightly, not wanting to make a noise, while crouching and moving at a fast pace. Once he is near the foundation in front of the warehouse, he finds his way to the rear of the abandoned structure. He jumps the rear part of the fence, making his way to the back door. It is boarded up with a piece of plywood. The way the boards cover the windows and doorway reminds Ricky of the safe house back in Flint. He knows the perfect way to knock down this door without making much noise. He takes out the bolt cutter Alex gave him and uses it as a wedge. He pops the plywood corner by corner slowly, not making much noise.

A few minutes go by, and the group starts to get anxious. "Is everything okay?" Ricky hears in his earpiece.

Ricky presses on his throat mic and whispers, "Yeah, just got this plywood door loose, now I'm entering the building. Over."

"All right, just got a little worried, that's all. You are taking forever, bro."

"Shut up, Ben, I'm trying to be quiet; now I'm making my way to the stairs. Over."

"'Ight. Over." Ben releases the button on his neck.

Ricky finds his way onto the top floor. The building has five stories. "I don't see a way onto the roof. I guess I'll just use one of these windows," he says to himself as he situates his rifle while positioning himself in the shadows of the building. He looks through the scope attached to the rifle at the main entrance of the warehouse. "I'm in place. Over."

"Understood, Ricky. Over." Alex points to James. "You are next."

James lets out a sigh. "All right." He gets out of the vehicle and walks at a fast pace around the corner, holding his rifle inside his baggy shirt and shorts in case he runs into any civilians.

It earlier occurred to James that a shortcut through the neighboring building of the warehouse would be ideal, although it was out of the question, as just about every building in the neighborhood was completely fenced in, and it would take too long to cut an entrance. He also considered jumping, but it would have made too much noise.

James completes his walk once he reaches the property he is tasked to enter. As he makes sure no one has spotted him, he approaches the premises. However, this building is not fenced but just locked with a padlock and chain. He takes out his bolt cutter and quickly cuts the lock and makes his way inside. It is an easier task than the one Ricky had to endure.

The building stands only three stories. James makes his way to the top. The roof has collapsed from the lack of maintenance, and the entire area is soaked with variously sized puddles of water. He uses the fallen pieces to get access to the roof, adjusts himself, and points his rifle toward the rear side of the warehouse. He then presses his throat mic. "I'm set."

Alex places his hand on Travis's shoulder. "You're up."

"Ooh-rah!" Travis tucks away his pistol and C-4. He imitates Ricky's route until he passes the backside of the building Ricky's in. Gradually, he analyzes where he is needed and cautiously advances to rubble that was once a building on the left side of the warehouse. He uses the ruble as shelter to stay out of view. Travis takes out the C-4 and readies it. "Set."

"Well, now it's my turn I guess." Alex looks at Ben. "I'll let you know when it's your turn."

"'Ight." Ben nods.

Alex exits the car with wire cutters in his hand. He crosses the street and makes his way to the fence. In a crouched position next to the fence, he puts his training into action. This won't be the first time he cuts a metal link barrier. He knows the right spots to cut to quickly create an entry hole without making any noise.

He cuts the metal wiring fence three times and pushes the barrier apart, making a small hole, which he crawls through undetected. He then tiptoes his way to another part of the barricade facing the right side of the warehouse, where he makes duplicate cuts prior to the last enclosure. The piece of the railing drops softly, and he adjusts himself to easily move toward the wall of the warehouse when it's time. "All right, your turn, Ben. Cross the street and walk past the warehouse, making sure the guards see you. Over."

"Ugh. Fuck. You better have my back, Ricky, and not get me killed. Over." Ben gets out of the car with his pistol on his waist, holding the AT4 inside his clothes. The night will make it hard to notice he is carrying anything under his shirt and make it look as if it is part of his oversize body.

"Don't worry, bro; I got this. They don't seem to move much, so I can pick them off easily. I've already done it a bunch of times in my head. Over."

"All right … here I go." Ben walks down the street, crossing the road. Directly in front of the warehouse, he stops to act as if he is tying his shoe. This gains the guards' attention fast. They start to speak Spanish, waving their automatic rifles at Ben, gesturing to him to keep moving.

Ben telling them he doesn't understand Spanish gains the attention of more guards inside the building.

The only guard that has been placed outside in the rear of the warehouse starts to move to the front to check out the commotion. Before he gets to the front, he spots Alex planting the C–4. The guard stops, and before he can utter a word, a cloud of pink mist leaves his head.

"Thanks, James; that was a close one. Over," Alex says.

"I'm a better shot than I thought. Over."

Travis finishes placing his C–4 and sneaks back to where he once was, outside the blast radius. "Thank God, James. Well, mine is a plant. How are you doing, Alex? Over."

One of the guards that is telling Ben to keep moving sees that he is holding something large inside his shirt, trying to keep out of view. "¿Qué es eso que usted está sosteniendo el interior de su camisa. Me muestres ahora!" The guard points to the rear side of Ben.

"I just finished," says Alex. "On my go." He hustles to the back of the warehouse, stepping over the corpse.

Ben hears that Alex and Travis are done and understands that the guard wants to see what he is holding. He knows it's finally safe to show the AT4. "Okay, okay, but you won't like it." Ben shrugs and commences to take out the AT4.

Before the guards can react, the five hear Alex in their ear. "Three … two … one. Go." Both sides of the warehouse blow, taking out anyone who was standing next to the walls. Ricky takes out the first guard with ease but shoots the second one, who was questioning Ben, in the arm. The guard falls to the ground in pain and lets out a yell.

Ben ignores the screech, points the AT4, and shoots the front entrance. Pieces of metal debris fly, and dust fills the air. Ricky finishes the guard off with a second shot to the neck. The guard starts to squirm around, holding his neck while making a drowning sound.

Ben drops the AT4 and takes out his sidearm. Alex, Ben, and Travis use the dust in the air as a smoke screen to enter the building. The three notice that the explosions have taken out most of the guards. Bodies of the enemy fill the floor of the warehouse. The guards that are still breathing are holding their amputated limbs dearly. These men are soon executed by Alex and Ben before they can realize what caused this tragedy.

The warehouse is empty and has nothing inside except the support beams and empty hospital beds with blood coating the sheets. Alex inspects a few of the beds and grins. He faces a hard truth when he sees handcuffs attached to every bed.

Ben catches up with Alex. "This must be where they hold the women before they ship them off.

Travis's eye catches two stragglers that survived the explosion running for cover. They try to shelter themselves in what seems to be an office space in the center of the warehouse. Travis sprints to the door they enter through, and before they can close it, he breaches their cover.

The pain from the shrapnel lodged in their bodies causes them to fall when Travis hits the door. One falls directly in front of Travis on his back, and the other falls right, on his stomach. Travis shoots the one that is in front of him between his eyes before he can aim his assault rifle. He points his pistol to the right of him and shoots the other in the leg and jumps on top of him, pressing his pistol to the guard's temple. "Move and I shoot!"

"No disparar, me rindo!" The guard goes limp, showing Travis he is no longer a threat.

Travis jabs his pistol into the guard's temple. "English!"

"Okay, I give up."

Travis gets up from the guard, not taking his pistol off him. "Get up slowly!"

Ben and Alex arrive with their weapons drawn as the guard is struggling to get up because of the gun wound to his leg and the shrapnel lodged in his lower back. His hands are pointed to the ceiling.

The three hear in their earpiece from Ricky, "Is everything straight? Over."

Alex presses the microphone that's strapped around his throat. "Yeah, No one's here. The blast killed most of the guards, but we killed the ones that survived, except one. We're going to interrogate him. And mom and our sisters—we think they were here. If so, we are too late; they have shipped all the girls. We are going to sweep more in this office space to see if we can find anything. Over."

Ricky looks through his scope down both sides of the road. "Fuck. Well, hurry up. Remember, we've only got a limited amount of time. Over."

"Understood. Over." Alex releases his microphone, presses his pistol to the back of the guard's head, and begins the interrogation. "Is there anyone else in this area?"

"No. Only *el jefe* was allowed in here unless someone was with him, and he's on the ground there." The guard points to the body of the many Travis shot, keeping one hand in the air.

Alex lowers his gun. "Ben, watch him. If he moves, kill him. Travis and I will sweep for any intel or evidence he is lying."

The office space consists of two rooms; there is a desk by the front door and a large freezer in the rear. Alex and Travis split up and search both of the rooms.

With caution, Alex enters the room. The room is empty except for a small desk and chair. He searches the drawers to find only emptiness. A small notebook is the lone item on the top of the desk. He skims through it. It consists of what seem to be the routes their cargo trucks take and all of the girl's names.

Travis enters his area with caution as well and quickly searches the room to find nothing. The place is empty. With Alex busy looking through the notebook he found, Travis moves to the large walk-in freezer in the back. He opens it and finds several nude bodies of men and women with faces that resemble those of kidnapping victims he has seen on the news. They have been held for ransom with their families still believing they are still alive. "Alex, you need to come check this out!" Travis starts turning bodies over to see whether any of the female faces look familiar. Each one has her neck slit from ear to ear.

Alex tucks away the book and runs to Travis. When he enters the freezer, he sees that Travis is on the last body. It is a female. When Travis turns her over, Alex runs over to the corpse, grasps the woman and cradles her body like a baby, and lets out a traumatized cry, uttering the name Brittany.

James, puzzled by the cry he hears from the warehouse, presses his microphone. "What was that?" he asks, hoping someone from the inside will answer.

"I don't know, James. Is everything okay in there?" Ricky looks through his scope, trying to see what is going on in the warehouse.

Travis looks away and walks out of the freezer. He runs out of the office space and locates a clean sheet. Ben seems puzzled as well. Travis runs back to the freezer and places his hand over Alex's shoulder. "I'm sorry. Here, she can come with us." Travis shows Alex the sheet. "Wrap her with this. We can bury her outside this place."

"No, it's better if she stays. The forensic team will look after her body until we are done finding my other family." A tear falls from Alex's eye. He wipes it away with the back of his hand "We are fine, Ricky and James. Well, most of us. We just found Brittany. She's gone."

Ricky grinds his teeth. "Fuck!" he yells at himself. "I told you, Mom, not to come … You're so fucking … Why didn't you listen … *God!*"

Alex covers Brittany's body. "We are leaving her body here. Our family will come for her when we are done. The police will hold all the bodies when they get here. Over." Alex walks to the front of the office.

Ricky grinds his teeth even harder as he comes to terms with the circumstances. "I guess that's for the best."

"You made it sound as if there were bodies other than the guards'?" James says through his microphone.

"Yeah, we found a freezer where they put the people they took and held for ransom," Travis responds as he walks behind Alex. "I guess they were keeping them frozen to make it look like they are still alive. But only Brittany's here out of the family."

"Those disgusting, nasty people," James says.

Alex snatches the guard by his hair and tosses him in the direction of the freezer. "Walk." He points his gun at the guard's back.

"Hurry up, guys; I hear sirens," James says.

Alex, ignoring James, shoves the guard into the freezer and points to Brittany's body. "Why her? Why did you guys kill her?" Alex points his gun in his face.

Scared for his life, the guard stutters. "So-some don't, how do you say, co-cooperate, and w-we kill them to-to show we are in charge of the others. She killed one of us by struggling. We had no choice."

Angered by his answer, Alex hits the guard in the top of his head with the butt of his gun, knocking their prisoner unconscious. "You piece of shit!" Alex yells in the unconscious man's face. "You're lucky I need you to decipher the notebook with the girls' names." Alex grabs him by his neck and drags him into the front part of the office. Alex takes a set of handcuffs that are on the front desk and cuffs the guard's hands behind his back. As he picks the man up and fireman carries him, he presses his throat microphone. "All right, everyone, go back to the car. Ben, Travis, pick up some of these rifles. We are going to need them."

The five men sprint back to the car. "Pop the trunk, Ben." Alex points to the back of the car. Ben gets into the car, pressing a button that releases the trunk and turns the car on. Alex whips open the trunk and tosses his prisoner inside. He shuts it and notices that everyone is inside the car. He runs and jumps into the vehicle. "Go, go, go!"

Ben takes off before Alex can shut the door. "Where are we driving?" Ben looks back at Ricky and Alex, then back to the road.

With eyes full of tears, Ricky says, "To the desert west of this city. We're going to kill this disgusting piece of crap. I don't know why you brought him."

Alex pulls out a book from his back pocket. "So he can tell us how to read this and drain him of any info he has."

Ricky frowns and pulls out the atlas. "Fine. But when we are done, I'm the one who is putting him down."

Alex confirms with Ricky. James looks in the rearview mirror to see smoke and lights from the police filling the night sky. The officials have finally arrived at the scene. "Who has the atlas? Show me where it is so I can tell Ben how to get there," James says to the brothers.

"It's easy; we don't need the atlas." Ricky rolls up the atlas and takes out his phone. "We are headed in the right direction; just keep going straight." He switches to his GPS on his phone and sets it to the outskirts of the city. "Just follow my phone and we'll get there." Ricky places the phone in between the driver and passenger seat. He sits back and stares out the window, holding back tears, reminiscing about his past with Brittany in silence.

CHAPTER 12

"THIS IS FAR ENOUGH. POP da trunk!" Ricky snatches one of the automatic rifles that were taken from the warehouse. He is the first to leave the car. He walks to the rear of the vehicle and whips the trunk open, pointing the rifle in their prisoner's face. "Get the hell out, now!"

Weak from the loss of blood, their prisoner rolls out and lands on his back, grunting in pain. Ricky sits him up and slams his back to the car. The others join Ricky, standing by his side. The men are facing the prisoner, watching Ricky hold his rifle's barrel in the face of their captive, his finger waiting on the trigger, ready to fire.

Alex takes out the book and drops it on the lap of their prisoner. He then squats to his eye level and turns the page to the names of his sisters and mother. They are all next to each other, with a line going through Brittany's name. "Where are these girls?" He points to their names. "The book says they are on one of three semi-trucks that left the warehouse. What semi-truck are they on?"

Nodding in and out of consciousness, the prisoner can barely read. He notices their names are in red ink. "*Rojo* means truck *dos*. They are on truck dos."

"Ben, get the atlas out of the backseat," Alex says.

"'Ight." Ben runs over and gets the book to hand over.

Alex opens it to a page that shows the east part of Mexico and points to the interstate the truck is to be driving on. "Is this the route the truck will take?"

"No." The man slowly traces the route the truck is taking with his nose. "No *peajes* … tolls."

Alex raises an eyebrow at the end of the route the man traced. "Okay, Veracruz? Why there?"

The man raises his head, trying to stay conscious. "We, Los Unos, have an airport in the outer city there." He takes a breath. "This is where they ship the *mujeres* all over the world to our clients that want to buy *ellos*."

Alex tightens his fist and gives the atlas back to Ben. "Now the truck; how can we tell it is the right one?"

With his strength drained, it takes a second for their prisoner to respond. "In the back of the book, their license plate number. Los Unos always has all-black *vehículos*. It's to show everyone so no one will mess with them."

"Okay, that's all." Alex releases his cuffs and walks behind Ricky, letting him get better aim on the guard.

The prisoner holds his gun wound and raises his free hand in front of Ricky's rifle. "Por favor, don't kill me. I can tell you more; just ask me. Please, *te lo ruego*." The man releases his wound and places his hands together as if he is praying.

Ready to pull the trigger, Ricky smiles with satisfaction. "That's all we need. Now die!"

"Wait!" Travis says before Ricky pulls the trigger.

"What?" Ricky looks at Travis angrily.

Travis has a puzzled look on his face. "This doesn't make much sense."

"What don't?" Ben asks.

"Los Unos are trained not to fear death." Travis looks at the prisoner. "Why are you scared?"

The prisoner drops his hands by his side. "Not all Los Unos are killers. If we can't make it in the training, we are set to be a smuggler or, how do I say ... a secretary?"

"I think we can use this info to our advantage. We probably could get more if we ju—" before Travis can finish his sentence, a loud bang sounds.

Ricky grins at the prisoner's dead body. "Now let's go. We don't have much time. We have to catch up with this truck."

James looks away in disgust. "Dude, why did you do that? Now we have his brains on the car."

Showing no remorse, Ricky steps over to the body, kneels down next to the corpse, stretches a piece of their victim's shirt, and wipes the bumper clean. He stands back up, eyeing Travis. "Let's go, I said." He gets back into the car, sitting in the passenger seat and awaiting the others. Ben and James follow immediately as always, entering the vehicle behind him.

Travis looks to Alex. Alex shrugs and enters the backseat of the car. Travis is in shock at the ruthlessness of Ricky's behavior, which he finds relatable to the personae of the many terrorists he dealt with in his past. Travis is the last to leave the scene, owing to the disarray of what just transpired, and he jogs to the car. James moves over to the middle of the backseat, and Travis enters.

Ricky looks in the rearview mirror at Travis. "He died before I pulled the trigger. I just wanted the satisfaction of putting a bullet in his head." Ricky looks away from Travis and gives his phone to Alex. Set the route we will take to catch this truck.

Alex goes to Ricky's GPS application and inputs the route. When finished, he places the phone in the center console between Ben and Ricky. "Follow the GPS, Ben."

Ben takes off, leaving the dead body under a cloud of dust and the night sky. Ricky takes out a USB cord from the glove compartment and plugs it into his phone so it can charge. "We don't even know how far they got. We could be hours behind the truck." Ricky looks down hopelessly.

Alex gives the notebook over to Ricky. "Look in the back, Ricky. It tells us the license plate number; how many guards are in the truck; how many women are in the truck; everyone's names, including those of the guards; when the truck arrived at the warehouse; and when it left. This book is gold."

Ricky squints and thinks. "We are only an hour and a half behind the truck. It must have been one of the semis that left the warehouse as we waited, right under our noses. How did we not see it?" Ricky bites his bottom lip in frustration. He picks up his phone to look at the route they are taking. "If we go over the speed limit by seven miles an hour, we won't get pulled over. And the man that we questioned also said the truck wasn't taking toll routes. If we did take them, according to my phone, it would be faster. We will catch up with the semi three hours from now, meeting here." Ricky shows everyone in the backseat the screen of his phone.

"That is right outside of Ciudad Valles." Travis sits back. "Good, just three more hours and I can get back to my wife."

Ben looks at Ricky. "We've got to stop for gas soon."

James looks at Ben. "We have to be fast, not to lose time."

"I got it, boss man." Ben salutes the rearview mirror, looking at James sarcastically.

James chops Ben in the side of his neck. "It's not the time or place to be a smart-ass."

"I see that the only rifles they have are AK47s, since they are the only guns you picked up," Alex mentions to Ben.

"Yeah, for some reason they only use AKs. Probably because it's most gangster or something like that. They had a lot of ammo on them too, so we are good with ammo and guns." Ben replies.

Thirty minutes later, they find themselves at a gas station next to the highway. Ben zips up his pants and walks out of the bathroom. He wobbles back to the car carrying a half-eaten taco he just bought. He takes the nozzle of the gas pump out of Ricky's car, and they get back to the highway.

"So when we see this all-black truck, what's the plan to stop it?" James asks the four.

"I've been thinking about this one." Ricky says before anyone. "I know, bro, you're the one with the plans, but this is just like a job we did not too long ago."

Ben looks to Ricky and then back to the road. "You talkin' 'bout when we robbed MOBB while they were driving."

Ricky looks at Ben. "Yeah. Everything will be the same, except we will be shooting."

Alex looks at Ricky. "Explain."

"We drive in front of the truck and slam on our brakes. The truck does either two things: swerve or stop. Either way, it slows down, so it won't do much damage when we take out the driver. By the time Ben presses on the brakes, we will have already taken aim on the driver and any others inside the truck. Once they slow down enough, we shoot the driver and everyone inside. We get out and swarm the truck. And the notebook says there should only be four guards on board, including the driver. We get in, recue our fam, we get out. Fast, just like last time."

"I'm impressed, Ricky," Travis says.

"Hey, like Alex said to us before, what we do on the streets is the same as you would do in the military. You guys just call it a fancy name."

"Perfect timing too." James looks to his phone and sees all the missed calls and tons of messages left by his child's mother. "My phone says we will arrive once the sun starts to show—five o'clock in the morning."

Alex sees that James has ignored the texts and missed phone calls on his phone. "Why so many texts and missed calls?"

"My baby momma, she always trippin'." He tucks the phone back into his front pocket.

"Oh," Alex replies.

Travis, not aware of how things work in the streets, asks James, "Does she know what you're doing?"

James shakes his head. "Nah. She's good. She don't need to know what I do. She just needs to stay home and watch the baby—you know, do her. She probably thinking I'm running around on her. I'll tell her what's up when I get back though. I can't have her and my baby girl on my mind when I'm out here, you know? So I put my phone on silent or shut it off."

Travis agrees and smiles, relating James's experience to what he goes through when he is shipped off while on duty. "Oddly enough, I know exactly what you're talking about."

CHAPTER 13

THE FIVE MEN LOOK OFF into the horizon in silence to see light peeping through the darkness and shadows of the trees on the mounting terrain. Tropical and desert trees surround them on both sides. Darkness is still in control of the hour, but not for long. The highway is empty.

"The sun is starting to show. We will be close to the truck soon." Ben looks into the distance to see whether he can spot an all-black semi-truck. "The GPS also shows we are thirty minutes away from the city the truck's going to."

James leans forward between the driver and passenger seats, closes one of his eyes, and looks ahead of him. "I see with my little eye that that you are right, Ben. You can barely see a city ahead. And there is the truck." He points.

Alex pulls back his rifle's bolt to check whether there is a round in the chamber. "Strap up." He takes off the magazine that was in the rifle to see how many rounds he has to shoot with before he runs out. "Twenty, including the one in the chamber; this should be good enough," he says to himself.

"Let's take a closer look at what's on the license plate. Don't want to make any mistakes and take control of the wrong truck." Ben squints and leans forward, placing his stomach on the steering wheel. "I can't see it. You've got better vision than me, Ricky. What's it say?"

Ricky looks to the back of the notebook and reads the license plate number on truck two. "L05-Z8-TA5," Ricky reads. He then looks to the back of the truck. "Yup, that's it. Let's take them out."

Travis points between Ricky and Ben. "Get ahead of the truck far enough that we can get a good view of everyone in the front."

"All right." Ben speeds up, slowly exerting more pressure on the gas pedal.

After checking how much ammo his rifle has, James lowers the middle part of the backseat and moves to the trunk. "Pop the trunk when ready and I'll spring out!" James says as he adjusts himself, speaking loudly enough that Ben can hear him from the luggage compartment.

"'Ight! I got you bro," Ben concurs.

Their car and the truck are now side by side. The guys keep their weapons out of view of the guards, so as not to alarm any of them.

Ricky counts how many are inside the semi. "I see three."

Looking unconscious, head against the window as if he is sleeping, Alex counts as well. Without moving his mouth, he confirms, "Yeah me too. The fourth guard must be in the back, keeping order."

"Shit!" Ricky says while trying not to show frustration.

"Looks like we have to move in faster than planned," Travis says.

"Let's do this." Ricky starts to roll down his window. "On my go this time. James, you get the driver; Travis, you get the driver as well. Two on the driver will make the odds greater. I'll get the dude in the middle. Alex, get the guy that's in the passenger seat."

Travis and Alex follow suit. For a brief second, the anticipation makes it seem as if time has stopped for all. The wind shudders through the car, and their ears pop from the vibration.

"Everybody ready!" Ricky shouts, looking back to see the team nod their heads. "Now!"

Ben presses the trunk button next to the steering wheel while stomping on his brakes. The trunk pops. Ricky, Alex, and Travis shift their bodies to aim behind the car, leaning out their windows. James hears an unlatching click and swiftly raises the trunk. The four have a lock on all three guards.

Trying to keep the car straight, Ben uses all his strength to keep the wheel from turning. The semi-truck does as planned. It swerves, trying not to hit the car while braking. The truck starts to head off the road and go down the mountainside. Before the front window leaves the view of Travis, James, Alex, and Ricky, they take their shots.

Gun sounds and the screeching of brakes echo through the mountains. Ricky shoots his man in the chest while spraying rounds from his rifle, hitting Alex's target as well. Alex shoots his mark in the head. James and Travis hit their guard several times while spraying their ammo, hitting the other two members in the process.

In pain from the bullet wounds, the driver lets off of the brakes and unconsciously gives the truck more gas. The truck speeds down the hillside, crashing into nature. It is soon stopped by the several trees and bushes it plows over.

Ben brings the car to a halt. James catches himself from falling out and gets his balance back. He is the first to get out of the car.

While getting out of the car himself, Alex reaches at Ben and catches his shirt, stopping Ben from advancing, and gives an order. "Get your pistol out and point it at traffic to tell them to turn around or stop. We need you to buy us some time. If they don't listen, shoot in the air." Alex sprints off, not wasting any time, to the semi to meet up with James. Travis and Ricky run side by side with Alex.

James reaches the truck first and ignores the sound of gunshots inside the trailer. He takes a hold of the clean, polished chrome door handle to whip the back door open. The sun reflects off the black paint of the semi, slightly blinding him.

Travis as well hears gunshots coming from the back of the truck. He instantly stops to take aim, looking down his sights with precise accuracy to have the jump on whoever is in the trailer. He monitors Alex and Ricky, who are still sprinting to the trailer, in his peripheral vision.

James begins to open the door and is surprised to catch the guard inside shooting the women in the trailer, one at a time. The guard turns and aims at James. Before James can lock onto his target, two gunshots are let out. James stumbles back from the force of the guard's shots making contact. James ignores the pain, situates himself, and aims in front of him, only to see the man who just shot him on the ground with blood coming out the back of his head.

James holds on to his arm where the bullets made contact. He looks back to see Travis lowering his rifle. "Holy shit," James says, in shock. *If not for Travis shooting him before he pulled his trigger, I would have been a dead man*, he thinks to himself.

Alex and Ricky finally make it to James. Ricky moves James's hand and inspects how severe the wound is. "It's not serious; just a graze."

Ricky hits James's back with an open hand. "Snap out of it. You should head to the front with Alex to see if any are still alive." He turns to Alex. "I'll check inside this trailer to release the ones still alive—and hope he didn't get to our sisters."

"Ten-four," Alex says as he starts to move to the front on the driver's side, keeping his mind right and not forgetting there still might be danger.

James gives Ricky an evil grin in response to the unsympathetic gesture he made toward his wound. In pain, James props his rifle on his shoulder, aims at the front side door, and moves forward.

Travis arrives at the back end of the trailer and leaps in before Ricky. He gives Ricky his hand and helps him up to begin analyzing the confined area. "It looks like he started killing them in the front, working his way to the back. He probably thought we were a rival gang. Not wanting to share any of these women, he was probably told to kill them if anyone tried to take control of the truck."

The women's arms are chained in the air. The chains are attached to the sides of the trailer. They all are sitting down with their legs crossed, potato bags over their heads.

Ricky walks to the first victim. "Why do you think the ones that are still alive are so quiet?"

"They're probably drugged and have no idea what's going on around them," Travis responds as he hangs back, too nervous to help reveal the identities of the deceased women.

Just as Ricky removes the first bag, gunfire rings out. Ricky looks to the road. It's Ben. The traffic is starting to build up, and by now it's obvious that someone has called the police. "We have to hurry up." Ricky finishes removing the first bag.

Alex notices that the trees the truck hit dismembered the three guards in the front. Blood coats the entire cabin. It appears that the middle guard did not have his belt buckled. His head is through the window, stopping at his neck. Twigs are protruding from one of his eyes. A branch of one of the trees is lodged in the driver's head, and the man that was in the passenger seat, with a bullet wound in the side of his head, somehow is missing an arm.

With the front cleared and the police coming in a matter of minutes, Alex and James hustle to the back of the trailer. They see that Travis and Ricky are removing bag after bag, not finding any of their family. Ricky is searching the left while Travis removes the bags on the right.

Travis realizes that the guard that was executing the women was in a hurry and shot each hostage just once in the head. He missed some of their heads and shot the sides of their necks, leaving them slowly dying.

Alex and James start to help. They both move to the back of the trailer, Alex on the left and James on the right, with the objective of meeting in the middle. Before starting his search, Alex frisks the dead guard and finds the key that unlocks the chains.

Alex unlocks the first woman. Her arms drop, and she rolls to her side. He takes the bag off to see her face. It's no one he knows.

Ricky moves to the next woman, who seems to be deceased. He takes off the bag. "Oh God, Mom!"

Alex hears Ricky. He stops unchaining the next woman and runs over to Ricky. He unlocks her chains. Ricky sees that there is blood on her bag, but there isn't a wound on her skull.

She looks up, dazed. "Mijos? Is it you?"

Ricky and Alex hug her for a brief moment and then stop to look at her face.

Alex feels he has something moist on his hand. "Yes, Mom, it's me and Ricky; we're here for you." He looks at it and realizes it's their mother's blood.

Alex and Ricky finish removing the rest of the bags, hoping they will run into the other two girls.

Ricky looks at all the faces. "The other two, they're not here!"

Ricky looks at James and then back to his mother. "Mom!" He adjusts her head to gain her attention. "Where are Stefani and Kayla?"

Anesthetized, Juana is hallucinating. She tries to snap out of it. "They killed her, right in front of us all!"

"Who?" Alex asks.

Juana rolls her eyes around, trying to focus. "Brittany." She begins to cry.

Ricky stands up after hearing another shot from Ben's gun. "We need to hurry. There is no time for this; we already know this." Ricky bends over to pick his mother up. "We will take her now, and when she sobers up, she can tell us."

"Stop!" Alex grabs ahold of Ricky's arm.

"Why?" Ricky stands up, looking at Alex. "We need to take her! We are running out of time."

Alex shows Ricky his hand, which is covered with their mother's blood. "When the guard was executing these women, he was in a hurry and was being sloppy. Our mother must have been the last to get shot before Travis killed him. He shot her in the bottom part of her neck, next to her shoulder."

"What!" Ricky looks at his mother's shoulder and sees blood.

"Judging by the angle of the shot," Alex replies, "the bullet is in her lung. She is dying, and there is nothing we can do about it. If we move her, she will pass by the time we make it to the car. The least we can do is be by her side until she closes her eyes. The drugs she is on must be making her numb." Alex looks down at Ricky kneeling next to his mother, clenching his fist. "She is in no pain," he says, trying to ease the heartache as tears trickle down.

"James and I understand the scenario; we will leave you to be here. We will go up and help Ben out." Travis respectfully steps around Alex with James following close behind him. James holds on to his arm, still with pain, picking up the dead guard's rifle.

Ricky stands up and punches the side of the trailer. "We are late again!"

Alex kneels down to his mother. "Mom."

"Mijo, is that you?" Juana struggles to look up at Alex. "Alex, I thought you were overseas fighting. You know I'm proud of you and your brother. I'm proud of all my children …" She rambles on.

Still facing his mother, Alex asks, "Kayla and Stefani, what did they do to them?"

"Stefani and Kayla?" Juana leans her head back to the wall of the trailer and closes her eyes.

Ricky kneels and taps his mother several times on the cheek to make her come back to reality. "Mom, where are Kayla and Stefani?"

She opens her eyes, and for a brief moment she snaps to. "Those pigs! I overheard them. They said they were too beautiful to be shipped to Europe, that the big boss man will like them. They were going to take them to his mansion in Saltillo." She stops talking for a few seconds. "I'm tired … I'm so tired. Why am I tired?"

"It's okay, Mom, you can sleep now." Tears continue falling down Alex's cheek.

"Yeah, Mom, it's okay." Ricky wipes a tear away with the tip of his finger.

Juana smiles and looks at the two brothers one last time, full of pride. She smiles. Her last breath is let out, and her pain is finally relieved.

Alex looks away as he shuts her eyes. Tears pour off his cheeks. Sorrow slowly begins to dissipate, and anger arises. He makes eye contact with Ricky.

The two brothers' eyes fill with hate. They both give their mother a kiss on her forehead. They tell her how sorry they are and how they regret not showing enough love toward her.

Alex speed-walks over to one of the women he previously set free and drops the key on her lap. "This key will free the other women. I would do it but I have no time. I'm sorry for everything."

They hurry and sprint out of the trailer, leaving their mother behind. They run up to Ben, Travis, and James, and give the motion to flee.

The men hurry up and enter the vehicle they are driving. As usual, Ben jumps into the driver's seat. The tires screech and they are gone, leaving behind white smoke, a wrecked semi, and a long line of traffic.

CHAPTER 14

"AHH!" RICKY SLAMS HIS FIST on the dashboard.

Ben hesitates to speak. "I know it's a bad time for you two know, but uh … when I was holding traffic up, people were recording me. They probably got what the car looked like. I told them to stop, and that's when I let out the second shot."

Alex wipes a tear from his eye. "The cops are probably right behind us as well. Pull into the next gas station."

Ricky hears the sound of wind inside the car. No one dares to make a joke or even turn the radio on. Alex takes out a bandage from his backpack and wraps James's arm up without saying a word.

Ben gets off the highway, and they make their way to the first gas station. It's small, run-down, and in the middle of nowhere. Ben puts the car in park in a side parking space, next to the station. "Now what?"

Alex looks to his left at Ben. "We need to get a new car."

Ricky watches a blue Dodge caravan pull into the gas station with only a woman inside. She looks to be in her late twenties; she has thin, long, straight black hair and very attractive.

"Pack up the guns and burn my car when I get out. We can't leave more evidence of who we are. We want the police to think, if anything, we are a rival gang." Ricky points with no emotion and certainty. "When she comes back out, we take her and the van."

Travis lets out a sigh. "I guess we gotta do what we got to do. But we do not harm her or I'm out."

Ricky looks over at Travis and then back at James's wound. "All right. I agree." Ricky is beginning to feel the importance of Travis and is no longer arrogant toward him.

Ricky reaches over Alex and opens the glove compartment to take out a rag. "When we pulled in, I looked for cameras. There are none that face outside." He rolls the rag up and gives it to Ben. "You know what to do."

Ben pulls out a lighter from his pocket and takes the rag from Ricky. He leaves the car and makes his way to the gas tank. He surveys the surrounding area to see whether anyone is outside. There is no one. He dips one part of the rag inside the tank far enough that gas touches the rag. He pulls it out and does the same to the other side. He gets the lighter ready and waits for Ricky and the others to charge the woman.

The rest get out of the car and look to the front door. Alex holds the duffel bag full of their gear. The lady walks out of the gas station holding a bag of sodas and snacks.

Just as she places her hand on the handle to open the door, Ricky grabs her at the waist and covers her mouth. Travis opens the side door, and Ricky throws her inside, including the bag of snacks. James takes the keys out of her hand while Ricky and Travis hold her down.

Ben lights the rag and sprints to the van. With the rag covered in gas, it takes only a second for the car to burst into flames. He returns to the van, where he is surprised to see that none of the others are in the driver's seat. After opening the driver's door, Ben acknowledges James's motion, and his immediate action is to insert the key in the ignition and start the van. He glowers, unamused to be driving again, puts the vehicle in reverse, and drives off, leaving all oblivious.

Ben looks to his rearview mirror and catches sight of the cashier standing outside, scratching his head, trying to figure out what just happened and why there is a car on fire.

Ricky and Travis are still holding the woman down, trying to keep her from doing any harm.

"Suéltame!" the woman screams through Ricky's hand, frightened for her life, with thoughts of them being part of Los Unos.

Ricky puts his finger up to his mouth, indicating for her to be quiet. "We mean you no harm." Ricky realizes she doesn't understand English. "Um, shoot." Ricky thinks of how to say he is no threat. "Amenaza! No amenaza. We are no threat."

She looks into Ricky's heartfelt eyes. "Tu Los Unos ?"

Ricky shakes his head. "No, we are not Los Unos."

The woman stops struggling. "Americano?"

Ricky places his sights on Travis to show him it's okay to release the woman. They both slowly stop holding her down. "Si," Ricky says.

The woman gets up and sits in one of the middle seats. "No español?" She looks at all of them.

"A little. Poquito." Ricky holds his thumb and index finger close together.

The lady thinks. "What do you want … *de mi*?"

Ben looks back. "Where we going, guys? I have no idea what way we are headed."

Alex points to the shoulder of the road. "Pull over to the side there."

Ricky closes his eyes to think how to translate his sentence into Spanish. "Mi familia." Ricky opens his eyes from the loss of concentration. "I don't know how to put it."

Alex steps into the conversation. "Los Unos took our familia."

The lady looks at them with concern and puts the broken Spanish together. She rubs her fingers together to show the universal gesture for money. "Americano means dinero. Lo siento. I'm sorry." She bows her head to show remorse.

Out of patience, James bursts in. "We need your van to go rescue them. Sorry, you have to come with us so you won't call the cops."

The woman has a puzzled look on her face. "Que?"

Alex realizes she didn't understand James. "We need your van to help our family. Necesito, vehículo, ayuda, familia." His Spanish is poorly put together.

"*No policía*, come with us, *ven con nosotros*." Ricky opens his palm to her for her phone. "We need your phone. Teléfono, por favor."

She finally understands and pulls out her cell phone and gives it to Ricky. "¿Qué pasa con mis hijos? My children? I cannot go."

"Sorry, we will let you go when we are done with the van." Travis shows her how sincere he is by placing one hand over her shoulder and looking into her eyes. "I promise you we won't harm you and will let you go when we are done with the van. We will even give you back the van."

Their hostage begins to loosen her tense body showing that she believes they truly mean no harm, but she seems to be confused by Travis's sentence. "¿dónde vamos?"

Slowly veering off the road onto the side, Ben ponders the sentence that their hostage just uttered. "What's that mean?" He looks behind him, at Ricky.

Alex looks at Ben to answer before Ricky. "She asks where we are going."

"Oh," says Ben.

Alex looks back at the woman. "We are going to Saltillo." Alex says, responding to the woman's question.

"Ay!" the lady sighs, knowing it's a seven-hour ride from Ciudad Valles to Saltillo. "*Por favor*, my children."

James thinks of his child and places his feet in her shoes. "We can't just let her babies be by themselves."

"Yeah, you're right," Alex agrees with James. "But what the hell do we do?"

"I've got an idea," Travis says.

"What?" Ben asks.

Travis gives Ricky an order. "Go to her contacts, Ricky."

Ricky abides the request. "What are we doing?"

Travis points to Ricky and Alex. "One of you, ask her to call someone who speaks English. We will tell them to look after the children, then hang up and toss the phone."

Ricky ponders this. "Hmm, 'ight. That will work." Ricky gives the phone over to the woman. "Como te llamas? What's your name?"

She looks at the phone, then back at Ricky, confused as to what is going on. "Felicia," she responds.

Alex points to her phone. "Felicia, llamada someone who habla Inglés."

Confused by the sloppy Spanish, it takes her a few seconds to understand. She scrolls down her contacts list and clicks the call button. Before placing the phone to her ear, James takes the phone.

"Bueno," the person on the phone says. Her voice is soft and innocent.

Assertively, James says into the phone. "Yeah, do you speak English?"

"Yes, who is this with my sister's phone?"

"That's none of your concern. You just need to know she is with a true American for a couple of hours. She will be home soon. She just needs someone to watch her kids until then."

"Ugh, this is just so typical of her. Well, you tell her to grow some cojones and call me next time and not let her boy toy do the talking for her as usual."

"Will do. Um, one more thing. The door is probably locked, so you will have to break in. Bye." James hangs up and tosses the phone out the window so their location cannot be traced. He looks at Felicia. "There, your kids are fine now."

Felicia understands a little of what has happened. "Gracias."

"Now that's out of the way, let's go. Where are we on gas, Ben?" Travis gazes at Ben and tries to check out the gas gauge.

Ben glimpses at the gas needle. "A little more than a half tank." He looks behind him at the four in the back. "Sucks she only went to the gas station for food. Guess we have to make a stop farther down the road."

Ricky opens his phone and switches it to the GPS. He types in "Saltillo," then gives it over to Ben. "Follow it."

Ben nods and places the van into drive, steadily moving back onto the road, which leads off into mountainous terrain.

CHAPTER 15

AFTER AN HOUR ON THE road, Ben's stomach starts to growl. "Yo, Felicia." Ben looks in the rearview mirror and points to the bag of snacks she was abducted with. "You think I can have some? I'm starving!"

Still angry at the unfortunate events, Ricky smiles a little, making a slight to brighten his spirits. "Ben, why you always hungry?"

The thought of Ben's obesity brings laughter to the vehicle. Everyone in the van laughs. Not understanding Ben's English but having a clear view of what he pointed to, she takes out a small bag of chips. "Si." She hands it over.

"Thanks," he says to Felicia, opening the bag with one hand while still steering. He ignores the fat jokes to keep the smiles up while merging onto another expressway.

Felicia looks at the number of the highway. She follows the number with her eyes with horror hyperventilating.

Alex sees her expression. "What's wrong? Que?"

"Los Unos, Son dueños de esta autopista," she says to Alex, her eyes showing deep concern.

"What was that?" Alex asks, not fully understanding the fast Spanish.

"It sounded to me like Los Unos own this highway," Ricky answers.

"Oh fuck!" Ben examines the road in frustration. "If I knew that, I wouldn't have gone this way. The GPS says it the fastest way. Shit!"

"This must explain why there is not much traffic. Well, anyways, it's all good. We can still ride. After all, we've got the firepower to take out any who want to stop us." James pulls out rifles from Alex's bag and hands one to everyone except Felicia and Ben.

Felicia's eyes widen. "Por lo que esta es la forma en que se va a salvarlos. Al principio pensé que todos eran tontos, yendo hacia ellos sin armas."

"What the hell. Did you understand?" Ricky looks at Alex.

Alex shakes his head. "No, that was too fast for me."

James speaks up. "She said, 'So this is how you are going to save them. At first I thought you were all fools, going toward them unarmed.'"

Travis pushes James in a playful manner. "So when were you going to say you speak Spanish?"

Ricky glares at James. "He doesn't."

James shows Ricky and Alex his phone. "It's an app I just downloaded. You speak into the phone, and it translates your language into a different language. It just so happened she said something right as I tried it." James presses on his phone's screen, and the phone plays Felicia's sentences in English.

"Hell yeah, boy," Ben says to James sarcastically. "Finally some use for you."

James is amused by the ridicule. "Whatever, Ben." He focuses on his phone and starts to scroll down. "I also can change the voice to a male's or keep it the British woman's voice."

"Do whatever you want. It makes no difference." Ricky answers James.

"I think I'll keep her voice. I'll name her Sarah. Sarah's a bad bitch. Aren't cha, Sarah?" James speaks into his phone, and it repeats his sentence in Spanish. Felicia laughs and shakes her head at James.

"You're a clown," Alex laughs. He takes out the magazine loaded in his assault rifle. "Since Los Unos only use AK-47s, they all take the same cartridges; let's split up the ammo." They empty the rifles, put all the shells together, and split the ammo up evenly.

Just as they reload the rifles, they spot three all-black SUVs on the opposite side of the road. The three SUVs slam on their brakes and cut across the median. They are now speeding behind the van, trying to catch up. The entire road occupied by these vehicles.

Ben stomps on the gas pedal and speeds up drastically.

"Here we go." James pulls back the bolt of one of the rifles to load it, ready for a fight.

"No need," Alex says as he takes out the rifle Ricky used before. He hands it to Travis and tosses the silencer next. "Remember, Travis knows how to plant C-4 and is good at long-distance shots. He is literally a military sniper and is the best I know."

Travis shows a presumptuous smirk as he screws the silencer on the rifle. "I'll take them out before they can get a better look at our vehicle and realize we have a clear shot at them." He places his attention on Ricky. "Do you know what the sights are set for?"

"Yeah, I set them at a hundred yards for my eye." Ricky replies.

"Okay." Travis turns the scope and moves to the front seat, adjusting Alex's location to have a better grip of Travis's legs. "They are about five hundred yards away now. By the time I get good aim, they should be three hundred yards away." Travis mutters to himself. He rolls the window down and props himself leaning out, sitting on the door and placing the rifle on the top of the van, aimed at the SUVs.

Alex gives Travis a thumbs up to assure him his grasp is strong. The vibration going through the car with an odd number of windows down overwhelms the men once more.

Not letting the noise of the vibration distract him, Travis looks down the scope and aims at the three SUVs. He establishes the trucks are side by side. He focuses on the front left tire of the far-right vehicle. He exhales and shoots once. A spark shows where he misses but gives an indication of where he must now take aim. Again he exhales and is exact. The tire deflates and shows sparks.

The truck loses control and rams the middle truck next to it. The sudden loss of control causes both vehicles to flip several times.

"Now only one left." Travis murmurs to himself as he slowly moves the rifle's crosshairs to the head of the driver of the last truck.

The driver seems confused about the incident that just happened to the left of him. Within seconds he realizes that the other two trucks just crashed and he must be under fire. Before he can react, a bullet pierces the front windshield and enters his face, going through his nose and out the back of his head, splattering gore. The SUV swerves off the highway and crashes into a tree. The vehicle comes to an abrupt stop from the crash. Survivors struggle to get out of the wreck.

"That takes care of them." Travis carefully reenters the van's window.

Ricky finally appreciates Travis's presents in their task. As Travis hands over his rifle back to Alex, Ricky smiles and gives Travis his blessing. "Three shots. Alex wasn't lying; you are good."

Travis smirks, full of confidence, and accepts the praise as Felicia claps.

"I'll keep this out just in case more want to try us," Alex says.

"We know your sisters are held in a mansion in Saltillo," Ben says with concern evident in his voice. "But that's all we know. We don't know what street it's on or even how it's guarded. And after this and the semi we destroyed, I'm sure they will be on high alert no matter where we go."

"Yeah, I was thinking the same," Alex agrees. "Maybe Felicia knows something about the whereabouts of the mansion."

Ricky points at James. "Get to your app and have it ask her if she knows anything about the mansion Los Unos owns in Saltillo."

"Okay." James takes out his phone, ignoring more of the text messages and phone calls that are on his home screen. "Man, I really need to tell my baby mama where I am before she flips more than she already has."

"Yeah, and I need to get a hold of my wife and tell her I'm okay," Travis adds.

"We also need to get some sleep. We all have been up longer than twenty-four hours," Alex says, piling more onto the list of requirements.

James speaks into his phone. "Do you know anything about the mansion in Saltillo that Los Unos owns?" He presses the button to play the words in Spanish and holds it up to Felicia's ear.

"¿Sabe usted algo acerca de la mansión en Saltillo que Los Unos poseen?" the phone states.

Startled by the app's capability, Felicia jerks her head away from the phone. "No se."

"Well, if she doesn't know, who will?" Alex asks himself out loud.

"Grandpa Mateo is from Mexico. He should know something. We can ask him." Ricky opens his hand at James. "Let me use your phone. I would use mine, but we're using it for the GPS."

"'Ight." James hands it over to Ricky.

Travis looks at James. "Can I use your phone when he is done to call my wife and let her know I'm not dead?" He chuckles.

"Yeah, right after I'm done speaking with mine," retorts James.

Ben tosses his phone to Travis. "I don't need to call anyone. I just texted my mom and let her know I'm straight. You can use it."

"Thanks!" Travis says to Ben as he starts to dial his wife's number.

"Ben, I'm sure by now you're sick of driving." Alex points to a ramp. "Get off here and go fill up at one of these gas stations. I'll drive for a few. We should take turns, letting us get at least a little sleep until we get to Saltillo."

Ben veers off and heads up the ramp. "All right."

"Is this cool?" Alex looks at the others to see them agree to the terms. "All right then, who is going to drive after me? I figure there is only five and a half hours left to ride. If we switch every hour, we at least get four."

Ricky points to the sky, holding the phone to his ear, listening to it ring. "I will. I'll go after you, bro."

"So it's settled." Alex points to the rest of the guys. "Travis, James, and Ben, you guys discuss among yourselves who is after Ricky. So on and so forth."

Ben pulls off the highway, stops next to a gas pump, and opens the door. Alex leaps over Felicia and Ricky and unlatches the side door. "I'll pump. You get some rest, Ben."

"'Ight, I won't argue." He enters the side door and makes his way to the back.

With thoughts of his last two living sisters, Alex heads toward the entrance of the gas station to pay. He looks up to the sky, where there is not a cloud in sight, and whispers to himself, "I pray you two are fine."

CHAPTER 16

"NAH, I SAID I'M FINE ... I love you too. See you soon." James ends his call. Leaning his head against the window, he shows a softer side of himself and smiles while slowly dozing off. He joins Travis, Ben, and Felicia in slumber.

"All right, Abuelo, love you. Bye." Ricky ends his call as well. His conversation consisted of asking his grandfather thirty minutes' worth of intense questions.

★★★

Mateo bows his head and places his phone on the hook. "I hope to god these evil men don't find out that Alex and Ricky are the ones doing all the craziness." Just as he finishes telling himself this, he hears the phone ring once again. "Hello?"

"I find it funny ... ever since you sent me those American girls, my business has been under attack. I pulled out a map and labeled every ambush. So far, it's every place those *maldita putas* have been. If I find out you had anything to do with this, I'm snapping my fingers, and your entire family is dead! You hear me?"

"Yes, yes, I swear it's not me," Mateo says, cowering at the sound of Mikhael's booming voice. "I don't know what you're even talking about. Anyone who would dare to attack you is not smart."

★★★

"Yeah, you're right. It's probably those Pitayas; they probably found out we have a nice selection of girls they want a part of." Mikhael ends the call by angrily tossing his phone across the room. "Mierda!" He stands up from his button-tufted executive chair and looks down at his wooden desk in exhaustion to focus on where he has marked all the attacks on a map in front of him. "They must be coming here next. Little do they know I'll have the city shut down, and any vehicle coming in will be *destruido*."

Mikhael walks out of his office. He opens the door and ensures himself that a guard is next to it. "Shut the town down. Tell everyone to go into their houses. If they are still outside in thirty minutes, kill them—no excuses! And if anyone drives into the city, shoot on the spot. Now go get the word out."

His goon bows his head, understanding the request, and quickly leaves Mikhael's sight without a word.

Mikhael walks back into his office. "My wives!" He says out loud. "No need to worry." He paces to a heavy set of decorated bifold doors. He opens them up with a smile of comfort, easing his tense state of worry. He walks up to Stefani and Kayla and places his hand on each of the girls' chins to show a cynical approach of endearment.

The girls cringe and try to move away, but the chains that are bolted to the wall keep them from moving an inch, and with their mouths strapped shut, all they can do is mumble the words they are attempting to scream.

"I won't let anyone harm you." He drops his hands from their chins. Satisfied, and using his sick fantasies for support, he walks from the closet, closing the doors behind him, leaving behind the squeamish girls. "Once these attacks are settled, we can consummate our marriage with no worries. Until then, sit tight."

★★★

Meanwhile, the brothers are still on the highway. Alex asks his older brother, flipping down the visor to stop the sunlight entering his vision, "So what did Old Guy say?"

"He said that six years ago, before the drug war hit the city, a group of Mexico's soldiers were hired by another cartel to take control of Saltillo. Well, after they took it, the cartel that hired the soldiers started to build a mansion. Soon after it was built, the soldiers that were hired took the mansion, and city over. They started their own thang after that. They called themselves Los Unos. Grandpa said they still use that mansion and that that is where the head honcho stays, safe and secure. Since he owns the city, he pretty much has his own army there."

"Hmpf." Alex thinks to himself for a moment. "Sounds like this is going to be complicated."

"Yeah, it will be," Ricky concurs. "Grandpa said there is a huge neighborhood in Saltillo, and a road called Calle Mandarina. It's a street right outside the neighborhood. We will be able to get to the mansion from there. The mansion sits on top of a mountain, overlooking the city."

Alex places his hand on his chin to envision how the mansion might look. "If it's on top of a mountain, based on my experience with reconnaissance, the rear side should be the most vulnerable. That's probably where we should strike. But this isn't like the small warehouse we invaded; we are going to need eyes from above to see everybody's movements without losing contact."

Ricky rolls his eyes. "Yeah, and how are you going to do that?"

"I told you, I've got connections, but we will have to do the hard work." Alex points toward Ben. "Get me his phone, please."

"Oh, right." Ricky shifts his body to the rear side of the van and pokes Ben's stomach. "Let me use your phone."

Ben stretches. "Time for me already?"

"No, give me your phone," Ricky repeats.

"Oh." Ben lifts his body to reach inside his front pocket. "Here you go." He hands off his phone and quickly falls back to sleep.

Ricky moves back to face Alex to hand over the phone. "Here you go."

"Thanks, bro." He scrolls the screen to the dial pad. "I'll take it from here; get some z's."

"Nah, my turn to drive is almost here. No point in sleeping."

"All right then." Alex dials into the phone and places it up to his ear to listen to the ring. "I think they would be done with the most recent mission and back on board the ship," Alex says to himself.

"You have reached Marine Corps Base Camp Pendleton," Alex hears. He pushes the number four before additional instructions are mentioned. The phone rings once again. A strong female voice says, "State your business."

"Security clearance number 107361; I would like to speak with Sergeant Rojas on the USNS-GW."

"Hold while I look up the clearance of the ship," the woman says sharply.

Alex yawns, stretches his back, and looks in the rearview mirror to see James and Ben snuggling. "Check it out, bro." He nudges Ricky.

"What?" Ricky asks, looking around.

Alex smiles. "Ben and James are snuggled with each other."

"Ricky laughs as he picks up his phone, opens the camera app, and takes a picture. "This is going on the internet." He switches it back to the GPS. "Oh shoot, I just remembered I need to enter the street." He inputs "Calle Mandarina, Saltillo, Mexico." The GPS changes but stays on the same route for now. Ricky places the phone next to Alex. "There, it should be straight."

Alex looks at the new destination on the phone. "Thanks, I forgot to mention that too."

"You have fifteen minutes. State your name?" Alex hears from the phone in his hand, which is still next to his ear.

"Understood. Name Boot."

"Boot?" She pauses a brief second at the name. "Okay I'll switch you over." There is a clicking sound and then silence. The phone sounds familiar to a disconnected line for a few seconds.

"Hello, Boot," Rojas speaks into the phone with confidence, aware the word "boot" is code for "Alex." "How's it going? Just left the briefing; we are sailing to base now." Rojas knows that the line is recorded so he must keep it casual.

"Good on your half, but not good on mine, I'm afraid. Remember how I mentioned I'd be in touch? Well, I need that favor. So far we have been unsuccessful even with Sergeant Baker with us. We need eyes like animals if we are to catch anything. I would say *eagle eyes*. I figured that with Sergeant Baker our task would be a breeze. But that's a negative. I'm no *eagle*." He continues to place emphasis on the word "eagle." "We need this. Find a way, please."

Rojas stays quiet for a moment. "Fine … I'll see what I can do. I'll call you back. Give me a number, and I'll contact you when I have a thorough plan."

"Ricky." Alex nudges his older brother.

"Yeah?"

Alex pulls the phone away from his ear and puts the phone on speaker. "What's the number to this phone?"

He thinks for a brief moment, "Eight, one, zero … five, five, five, two, eight, two, nine."

"You get that, Rojas?" Alex says, requesting confirmation acknowledgment.

"Yeah, I think. The area code is 810. And the rest is 555-2829?"

Alex looks at Ricky to confirm that the number is correct. Ricky nods. "Yes, that's affirmative," Alex says into the phone, taking it off speaker.

"Okay, I'll be in touch." Rojas ends the conversation.

Alex tucks the phone inside his pocket. "I'll hold on to the phone for now; he should call me back on a blocked unknown number in a couple of hours." Alex pulls over to the side of the highway. "It's about time to switch. You're up, bro."

"All right." Ricky gets out of the van and switches places with Alex.

The brothers simultaneously shut the vehicle doors they are located next to. Alex adjusts himself next to Felicia. Ricky merges back onto the highway while opening a soda pop Felicia bought and taking a drink. Alex closes his eyes and falls fast asleep with ease as a result of a lack of rest. Resting in uncomfortable situations is all too familiar with him. Ricky is left alone with everyone asleep. He will be in his thoughts, fighting off his inner demons, for the rest of the hour, becoming ever wiser.

CHAPTER 17

A FEW MINUTES LATER, ALEX is awakened by the phone vibrating in his pocket. Before he can pull the cellular device out, he stops upon realizing that a woman is driving. He takes a second glance to snap out of his tired state of mind and become completely awake. His double-take proves he is correct. He fully comprehends that Felicia is the one driving while James is behind her seat with his legs propped on the armrest and his hands behind his head.

"You're doing good, Felicia, keep it up." James stuffs his face with children's fruit snacks that were intended for Felicia's children.

Alex shakes his head at the scene and answers the phone. "Hello?"

"This is Rojas. We are on a secure line now, Hernandez."

"Okay, good."

"I meant what I said before you left us—'I will do what I can to help you.' Well, I did just that. I didn't know what else to do, because I needed a high-ranking position or security clearance to get inside the ship's satellite system. And you and I both know I am no officer."

"True." Alex raises an eyebrow with anticipation as to what Rojas will say next.

"I told the captain your situation and asked whether we could use the United States satellites."

"What did he say?"

"He said only under the jurisdiction of the Pentagon would we be able to use it, unless I stole the card key from him. And if I did that, I would have a ten-minute window to help you before others came in and arrested me for treason. Then he told me where he kept the card in his office and walked away."

"Shit. It's okay; we can do a few hours of reconnaissance before we move in and hope the inside is not as heavily guarded as we expect it to be."

"You know I'll take a bullet for you. You're my brother. And to save your family, I think it's messed up that our government won't let us help one of our own without being labeled with treasonous intentions. I guess this comes down to my human morals. I'm in. And judging by the tone of the captain, he is as well. But he just isn't willing to get caught. I don't care if I do."

"Are you sure you're in?" Alex asks, feeling some hesitation in knowing he has placed one of his brothers in arms in a tight situation.

"Yeah, just let me know when you're in place, then I'll take the card from the captain and make my way into the satellite room."

"Certainly." Alex looks at a sign they just passed. "By the looks of a sign I just read, we are in the city limits already. So I'll call you back on this number you called me from when we are set. It should be soon."

"Okay, I'll be waiting." Rojas disconnects.

Alex drops the phone on Ben's stomach to wake him. "Wake up, everyone; we are getting close to our destination." He looks to the road and establishes that they are getting off the ramp and turning onto a street, bringing them ever so close to their task.

They stretch away their tiredness. Ben conceals his phone into his pocket. Travis rubs the sleep from his eyes, and Ricky ponders the situation James has Felicia in.

"I should have thought of that," Ben comments with a laugh, noticing James making Felicia drive rather than him.

Ricky scowls at James, unamused. "Yeah, it's something I expect from you, Ben, but not James."

"Shoot, everyone knows I'm lazier than Ben. Just cuz I'm skinny don't mean nothin'." James looks back at Ben and Ricky with a smug smile.

The city operated by the cartel is not as run-down as Travis expected. He reads off Ricky's phone. "It says we are ten minutes from our destination. I guess they like to take care of the neighborhood so close to their mansion. Also, I find it strange that there is not a civilian in sight."

"This city is owned by Los Unos, everyone probably left or was killed," Ben says, assuming the worst.

Felicia extends her index finger at James to obtain his attention. She holds her hand to her head as if she is on a phone. James concludes she wants the translator on. He switches to the app and transfers the phone to her. She says "¿Crees que nos van a notar." The phone then states, "Do you think they will notice us?"

Ricky studies the van to see how inconspicuous it is. He reassures Felicia by shaking his head.

Ben cracks his back by twisting from left to right, overconfident in their situation. "The only way they will figure us out is if they are looking for a soccer mom." He chuckles.

"Yeah, we are not conspicuous in the least. We are fine," Travis says, adding to Ben's self-assurance.

James leans forward to the front windshield and squints to see what seems to be a man on the horizon. "What's that? What's he doing?"

"RPG!" Travis screams.

Alex yells, "Everyone, jump out now!" He clasps his duffel bag full of equipment.

Ben releases his gun quickly, clutching ahold of Felicia and rolling out of the moving vehicle. He uses his soft, squishy body to shield her from the impact of the road.

The empty van coasts a few yards into the rocket just shot by the antagonists and blows up. Parts fly in different directions, some of them nearly connecting with James. What looks to be a military militia starts to appear over the skyline.

Ricky points to a two-story house in the middle of an open dry field. "Everyone get in there now!" he screams.

They follow Ricky's order without question and sprint to the house. Ben grasps Felicia's hand and pulls her to the house.

Leading the way and approaching the house first, Ricky attempts to turn the doorknob. It's locked. With all his might, he kicks the knob. The door whips open. The group rushes in like ants enter their hole when it begins to rain.

"Everyone, start barricading the windows and doors!" Travis shouts.

Too scared to move, Felicia stands in one spot with a blank expression on her face. James is first to realize this. "Move, girl!" He clenches Felicia's arms and starts to shake reality into her.

She widens her eyes and snaps out of the daze. "Okay, okay." Felicia begins to help barricade them inside. The new recruit takes a chair from the dining room table located in the corner of the room to stack on top of the other household items arranged against the rather large living room window.

"What was that?" Travis hears a door open from under their feet. "The basement!" He quickly moves downstairs and stumbles upon the homeowners running through the basement door that leads outside. A middle-aged man and woman dart down the street. He hears several pops, and the two homeowners drop to the street, having been mowed down with bullets. Travis turns his head out of sorrow and closes the basement exit. He uses the bolt that is attached to the door to secure the passage. Anything that is in view is placed adjacent to the door. Once he feels it is heavily enough barricaded, Travis swiftly makes his way back to the others. "Basement is complete. The homeowners ran off but were killed by weapon fire."

Alex rubs the back of his neck in frustration. "Shit, I don't want anyone else to get hurt!"

Ben and James come down from the upstairs, searching for any vulnerable spots the enemy might use to enter.

Ben wheezes from having to move at such a fast peace. "No attic, but the windows are covered," he says.

"How the hell did they find out we were coming?" Ricky asks out loud.

"My thought is that they must have realized the pattern of destruction that was occurring and set up this trap. Crap!" Alex says, sounding worried.

"No matter, we can still do this; we just need to keep them at bay while taking them out slowly." Travis looks around, studying the house.

"Yeah, and how do you plan us holding off an army with limited ammo and a house made of clay?" Ricky retorts sarcastically.

"Stop. This is no time to argue or panic," Alex interrupts. "We still have Rojas. It might not look like it, but we have the upper hand. For this to work, I need eyes in the front and the back from the upstairs.

We need someone to watch the basement entrance as well. Also, I need two to stay on the main floor to watch for threats trying to enter from the left and right of the house. Until I find out what this eagle can do, this will be our post."

Travis volunteers to be a sniper upstairs. "Since I'm good with long distances, I'll go up."

"Same here," Ricky says while grabbing the other rifle with a scope attached.

"Okay then, it's settled," Alex says. "Travis, Ricky—upstairs. James and I are on the main floor. And Ben, since you have no weapon, get in my bag and take out my KA-BAR. You and Felicia are downstairs. It's safest there, but we still need to be aware."

"All right, this sounds secure." Ben says, pulling out the large knife from the bag. "Vamos," he tells Felicia. Without much hesitation, she follows Ben downstairs.

"I'm calling Rojas!" Alex yells to inform the others.

"About time," Ricky responds to Alex. "Hurry up; we are going to need him quickly."

There are a few rings before Rojas picks up. "Is it time?"

Alex walks to his window and places his rifle on the ledge at the best possible location to fire from while not being spotted easily. "Things didn't go as we expected."

"That's what always happens," Rojas replies. "What's going on? What happened?"

"They were expecting us, and now we are pinned down in some vulnerable house in the middle of an open field." Alex lets out a shot from the rifle to fend off the enemy.

"Any casualties?" Rojas asks.

"Only the homeowners so far; they took off when we entered. I think they thought we meant harm. Our enemy killed them on the spot with gunfire."

"We need to stop this before anyone else gets hurt," Rojas says through the phone, breathing shallowly as if he is pacing fast.

"Do you have any ideas?" Alex asks.

★★★

On the upper deck, Rojas catches a glimpse of the large body of water he is sailing on, inhaling the humid air, just before walking into a long white hallway with a heavily secured door at the end. "Yeah, I have one, I think. Just give me a second. I went ahead and already stole the key card, thinking it wouldn't take much time for you to call. I'm entering the room now." Rojas pulls out the key card from one of his pockets and scans it. The heavy metal door unlatches. Rojas pushes the entrance free. He observes several sedentary soldiers behind computers, monitoring several locations across the globe. He holds the card up in the air and speaks loudly enough for all to hear. "I'm Sergeant Rojas, and one of our own has had family abducted and is facing imminent danger and is cornered! I am risking everything right now to help him survive. Our government wasn't taking action, so he took action into his own hands, as many of you would! This card I hold should bypass all security protocols, ensuring no alarm will sound from tampering. I ask you to please allow me to take control only for this short time. With your help, we can do the impossible and save our own when all odds are against him. Blaming me for this treasonous act will be easy. Tell them I forced everyone by taking everyone hostage. Please help him. Help my brother—our brother."

All attention is focused on the card in Rojas's hand. They began to discuss the matter among themselves, and within seconds they all come to the same conclusion. They give him full cooperation, knowing that everything can be bypassed and nothing can fall back onto them.

Suddenly a woman who seems to be in charge stands to attention. Her stature is very masculine. Her name tag reads "Jones," and her uniform is in the best condition Rojas has ever seen. Rojas is sure this woman holds her occupation with the utmost importance. "What's your first order, sir!"

"All eyes to Saltillo, Mexico!" Rojas speaks out.

"Yes sir." The woman positions herself back at her seat. "You heard him!" she says to the rest, who are behind computers.

Rojas puts the phone back to his ear, "Any idea of your exact location?"

"No, but we are heavily surrounded by soldiers. There're around a hundred men out there. I'll scour the zone." The ear-splitting sound of

Alex discharging his weapon to keep their foe from advancing muffles the phone call.

Rojas lowers the phone from his ear. "Switch to thermal and find where a cluster of soldiers are located."

A voice speaks out from the corner of the room immediately. "We found something, sir."

"Pull it up to the main screen," Rojas commands. He monitors closely and registers a vast halo of people encompassing a house that has six others inside. He positions the phone up to his ear and starts to speak to Alex again. "Are there six of you in what looks to be a two-story house?"

★★★

Alex inspects dust entering the house through the deteriorating siding, with the sound of a long whistle following. "Yeah, that's us," he answers while the floor cracks and pops as he and the others make themselves more comfortable. Some hide in the shadows if possible, using the items they barricaded each other in with as a shield. James, Travis, and Ricky keep a close eye on the enemy enclosing the house, trying to conserve ammunition as well as holding fire upon their enemy, delaying the inevitable at as far a distance as possible. The brothers and their group are a safe enough distance from any gunfire from their enemy so far.

Unexpectedly, the militia stops progressing toward them. A voice speaks out from a megaphone: "Hola, mi nombre es Mikhael, no sé quién eres, o por qué nos atacas antes, pero solo sabemos que te mataremos si no te rindes."

Ricky grinds his teeth. "That must be the leader. He's lucky he went too far, or I'd end this right now."

"Easy, Ricky," Travis replies, overhearing what he said to himself. "We will get him eventually."

★★★

"Okay," Rojas says, "now that we located you, I'll zoom out and count your enemy." Rojas lowers the phone from his ear once again. "If the boys are in that house, how many surround them?"

"One hundred thirty-six men armed with automatic rifles," a voice speaks out. "With five of them holding RPGs as well."

"They're not too protected; they're just out in the open." Rojas rubs his chin in thought. "Do we have any air support near them?" he asks.

"Yes, sir," Sergeant Jones quickly answers. "We have two armed Predators hovering over Mexico. One is ten minutes away from them, and the other"—she looks back down to her computer to double check—"fifteen minutes away."

"Good. Send them both to destroy the threat," Rojas commands.

"One concern, sir." the sergeant replies.

"What's that?" Rojas looks at the woman.

"It will be danger close; the blast might impact the house."

Rojas takes a second. "Send them. It's their only chance." He brings the phone back to his ear. "Boots? Hernandez?"

★★★

"Yeah, I'm still here," Alex replies, viewing the militia in a complete halt.

"We have two Predators that have been collecting information on Mexico for some time now. They are fully loaded and ready to go. Estimated arrival time, fifteen minutes. Danger close."

"It will have to do; I think the leader is giving us a surrender speech."

"Te daré cinco minutos para responder, pero no, si no lo haces, encontraremos una manera de entrar y no mostrarás misericordia!"

"What is he saying?" James asks Alex.

"Yeah, I don't understand!" Ben speaks from the basement listening closely to everyone.

"It kind of sounds like he is giving us a few minutes to surrender," Alex replies with his rifle pointed out the window and with the phone still up to his ear, using his shoulder as leverage.

"Yeah right, if we surrender, everything will have been for nothing," Travis says. "And I'll be damned if I left my honeymoon just to be captured by these idiots."

"I'll have the Predators lock on to the surrounding threat soon, and my job will be done," Rojas vocalizes into the phone.

"Thank you, Rojas. I owe you big. But one more thing."

"What's that?"

"Mikhael, the leader of Los Unos—tell me, have you heard anything about him?"

Alex can hear Rojas say with his mouth away from the receiver, "Pull up Mikhael's records, first in command of the cartel titled Los Unos." He then begins to read from the main screen. "Wow, he is wanted by the United States and the Mexican government … For drug trafficking, kidnapping, murder, slavery, and women trafficking. When you kill this bastard, you won't only be doing yourself a favor, you will be doing the world one as well. He's a scumbag!" Rojas takes a step closer to the screen to analyze the description further in detail. "It shows why he hasn't been captured yet. He has many connections with several different people. It seems they all are under his jurisdiction. Most of the police task force are among these people. It's impossible to arrest him using the law. There's a lot more info on Mikhael and the wicked deeds he has done. You need me to tell you more?"

"No thanks, that will be enough. This gives me a little more reinforcement to put one in his skull." Alex grits his teeth. "Thanks again for your help; our end would be soon if not for your sacrifice."

"Don't mention it."

★★★

In the command room, Rojas hangs up the phone. "Okay I want both of those Predators locked on the threat. Take out as many men as we can."

"It's already done," Sergeant Jones says.

"Now we wait and hope they can hold off until the drones arrive," Rojas mumbles while keeping a close eye on the screen.

CHAPTER 18

"FIFTEEN MINUTES AND AIR SUPPORT will arrive!" Alex yells. His companions cheer.

Knowing the fight might come to an end soon, Ricky begins to have a sudden thought of guilt. "Hey Travis!" he shouts down the hall into the other room.

Travis replies without taking his eye away from his scope. "Yeah, what's up?"

"Sorry that my brother asked you to be away from your honeymoon!"

Still in the same potion as his fellow peers, keeping his eye on the threat in his crosshairs, Travis realizes what Ricky is trying to do. "That's not really an apology, but I'll take it!" he says with a laugh.

"What do you mean?" Ricky asks, sounding frustrated.

Alex suspends the conversation, hollering up to the second floor. "You're trying to apologize for being a dick, but you apologized for me, you jackass."

"Well, I guess that's all I can do," Ricky responds complacently.

"That's a lot coming from this guy, Travis. Trust me, I know!" James says, mocking the conversation.

Travis laughs out loud. "I'll keep that in mind, James!"

Ricky undermines the conversation. "Man, whatever!"

Soon their concentration on the battle overwhelms the household. Conversations turn to quiet. Eerie silence surrounds the house. The group inside understand that surrender is out of the question; even if it were possible, there is a high risk decapitation would come after.

Minutes pass, and Mikhael is handed the megaphone once more. "Your time is up!" He says in a deep accent "Entonces, ¿qué va a ser?"

The brothers don't move an inch. Their fingers tighten on their triggers keeping an eye on the closest target, waiting for the enemy to get into range.

"Okay? Que así sea. So be it!" Mikhael waves his hand, signaling two men to progress toward the house.

The two soldiers are armed with rocket-propelled grenades being carried on their shoulders. They proceed, aiming at Ricky's general area in the house. Ricky slowly exhales with one of the men in his crosshairs. Before inhaling, he pulls his trigger twice before recoil takes his accuracy. Both of the men fall out of his sight.

Mikhael yells out with anger. He commences to thrust his hand upward furiously, moving it in a circular motion. The three that are left holding RPGs move in from different directions, one each coming toward Ricky, Alex, and Travis's locations.

"Don't let them fire anything!" Ricky screams out. "Take them out before they get into rage."

Three pops come from the house, and the men holding the RPGs fall to the ground. Two try to stand but are executed before they get close. One of the three slowly shifts, so sluggishly none of them comprehend the soldier is moving. His body lies in front of Alex's post.

As the man pulls the trigger from his rocket launcher, Alex shouts, "Shit!" and jumps away from the blast. Shards of clay debris from the house land on Alex's back.

James falls from the blast. He rubs his eyes and gathers his senses back. "Fuck!" James double-takes and positions his body in a more stable form. He observes a shockingly huge hole in the house. Having no choice, he sacrifices his post, leaving him vulnerable to attack, to provide assistance.

Mikhael's men take advantage of the blast to swarm the hole. Alex and James use all their might to fend off the enemy.

Alex digs through his bag and pulls out the last of his C–4. "I've got something for them. Keep suppressing fire!" He positions the explosive compound beside the opening and decides to trigger it when the militia enters the house. After it's set, he joins James in firing at their opponents once again, executing one after another. The wave of men seems endless. "I'm good now; you can go back to your position, James!" Alex calls out through the gunfire.

James nods and hustles back to his role in a crouched position, trying to stay out of the cross fire. "Oh shit." James glances through the window and sees that the cartel took advantage of the time when no weapon fire was coming from his side of the house. The wave is now stepping away from the window. He holds the trigger down, knowing there is no longer a need for accuracy, as every bullet will make contact. His grunts echo over the tumult.

The blast and gunfire from above startles Felicia. She hides behind some old boxes filled with the homeowners' knickknacks and decorations.

Ben walks over to her while on high alert and tries to comfort her. "It's okay, we will get out of this. We can do this. I know it."

A rather large masked man dressed in a military uniform identical to those of the others that are charging the house makes his way through the gunfire to the basement exterior door. He uses his strength to disassemble and open it. In the process of ramming the door open, all the items that were barricading it plummet, making an unusual noise among the firefight occurring above.

Ben hears the off-putting noise and checks the situation out. To his surprise, he spies the rifle in the soldier's arms, and he hesitates. Just then the weight of a heavy object in his hand reminds him that a knife was given to him. As the man begins to aim his weapon, Ben slings the knife at his combatant. The man ducks and is missed. He catches his balance after ducking, but Ben dives at him, grasping the rifle his adversary holds. A game of tug-of-war commences. Eventually the two fall to the ground. Ben uses his weight to his advantage and rolls on top of the man, taking the wind from his lungs.

Ben finally rips the gun away from his challenger. With no other weapon on hand, Ben's enemy frees his legs from under Ben and knees Ben in the groin. Ben falls over to his side, in pain, and the man easily recovers his rifle. Just as Ben recuperates from the pain, he looks up to see the barrel pointing at his eye.

"Morir," The man says.

At that moment, Felicia stabs him in the back of the head with the knife Ben threw. The shock that is sent through the enemy's body causes him to squeeze the trigger. Bullets miss Ben's face by inches, and he falls with a shocked expression on his face.

Ben rubs his ear from the ringing and looks up at Felicia's face to witness the horror that she is expressing. He stands and hugs her with great gratitude, picking her off her feet. He then releases her from the hug and thoroughly does a body check for them both. "No bullet wounds, that's good. Now let's shut this door and this time put more against it."

"Crap!" Travis yells out.

"What?" Ricky replies.

"They have a convoy truck full of men with a metal plate covering up the windshield and a plow attached to the front. They are driving straight at us." Travis shoots at what he can. Firing at the tires and the engine doesn't make a difference; it still races toward the house with full force.

"Take it out!" Ricky responds.

"I did what I could; it's no use. It's still coming at us." Travis pulls back his rifle from the ledge. "We have to go to the basement. It will be our only cover after the destruction!"

Ricky shoots one more time and sees Travis going down the stairs in the corner of his eye. Ricky pulls his rifle from the window as well and follows. "Basement, now!" Ricky yells to James and Alex as he passes by.

Alex and James pull back and follow as well without question. They rush to the back of the house where the entrance to the basement is located. They all hustle down the basement stairs one after another. Just as they descend the last step, the truck bulldozes its way through the back of the house and stops inches away from the C-4 Alex placed.

Ben feels the house shake. "What was that?" He and Felicia stop placing boxes and totes against the door that leads outside.

"A truck full of men smashing its way through the house," Travis replies.

The noise of several soldiers jumping from the vehicle vibrates through the floor above them. Footsteps hover over their heads.

"Shit, now what?" James asks hopelessly.

"Now they point their rifles down and fire through the floor, killing us," Ricky says sarcastically.

Alex waves everyone away from the blast radius of his C-4. "Not yet." He points up. "Wait for it."

"Wait for what?" Travis asks.

"Alex placed C-4 next to the first hole they blasted," James answers.

"Oh shit!" Ricky says as he braces for an explosion with the others.

There is a tremendous bang, and the explosion sets Felicia and the others on the ground. A large hole is left in the floor where Alex placed the C-4. The explosion leaves half of the house collapsing inward on what remains of their opponents. Loud grunts of pain emanate from the rubble. Pieces of their limbs have been ripped off from the explosion. The bodies are pinned down by large chunks of the house and truck.

"Ugh." Alex tries to recover from the explosion, looking up to the floor above him, holding his shoulder while lying still. He sits up and oversees the others as they regain their strength after the blast.

Travis glimpses around. "Now we have no way in or out. I don't even see a way to point our weapons at our enemy surrounding us. We are trapped in this basement."

James agrees after trying to find a way out as well. "Yup, we are trapped."

The back half of the M35 military truck the enemy used to ram the house is a few feet from them. It barely missed landing on top of them when it fell through the floor.

Ben helps Felicia to her feet. "I guess this is a good thing. No way for them to get us."

"I guess it is … unless they find a way to toss grenades down here," Ricky says, unsure of their scenario.

They start to hear voices above them and pieces of the house moving.

Felicia points to the floorboard above them. "Que ese so?"

"They are digging up their people and trying to get to us," Alex answers. "What do you think?"

"No," Felicia says, making it clear Alex didn't understand her. She points to her ear. "Escucha."

"Oh shit." Travis looks up. "That sounds like jets, or in this case the Predator, and if we can hear it, that means it already flu … Everyone down!" Travis drops to the floor, covering his head.

A vicious wind rips off what was the roof, and everyone falls to the floor once more.

★★★

"No!" Rojas yells out, looking at the screen. His view from the satellite shows a huge crater next to what used to be the house. "We shouldn't have locked the Predator to their enemy, but to a location near the house. I wouldn't have ever guessed the house would fall in and the enemy would be directly on top of them."

The doors of the satellite room open, and several military police storm in and tackle Rojas to the ground.

"What's the meaning of this?" Sergeant Jones asks, standing vigilant.

"He had unauthorized clearance to this room," one of the MPs states.

Ignoring the thought of being captured, Rojas is concerned only with the disaster. "I have to see if they are still alive." He tries to struggle free. "Switch to thermal!"

"Disregard that order," an MP tells Sergeant Jones, shaking Rojas by the arm to get a better grip.

Ignoring the MP, she switches the satellite. "They all are alive, all producing heat signatures that show strong life."

The MP looks at her with much displeasure.

"Oh, thank god." Rojas says as he loses strength in his legs and is hauled out of the room.

★★★

"Is everyone okay?" Alex asks while studying his surroundings, astonished to find no floor above them.

"I'm fine," Travis says, brushing himself off. "If it wasn't for us being in this basement, I think that blast would have taken us out as well."

James pushes off a huge piece of the roof that is lightly on top of him. "I'm good."

"Yeah, it looks like everyone is straight." Ricky remarks as he dislodges a nail from his left hand.

Alex limps over to Ricky and places his hand on his shoulder. "Are you sure? That looks nasty."

"Yeah, I'm good." Ricky drops the nail and starts to search around as well. "I think you're right, Travis, if not for us being down under, we'd be screwed." He tears a section from the bottom part of his stained shirt to wrap his hand.

Felicia tries to stand up but drops back down from pain. "Ayudame!"

Ben rushes over and inspects the damage. "It looks like one of the axles from the truck dropped on top of your ankle."

James rushes over to help Ben raise the piece off of Felicia. "Can you walk?" James asks.

Felicia holds out her hand to Ben so he can help her stand.

Felicia attempts to walk on her bad foot. "Ay, no!"

"Well, it looks like we have to pack you from here on out." Alex points to Ben. "Since you seem to have a thing for her, you can carry Felicia."

"What? Wait, do I? Yeah, I guess so," he chuckles. Ben looks at Felicia with a smile, rubbing the back side of his neck.

She smiles back, forgetting the pain for a brief second.

"There is no time for this." Ricky gets between them and moves them both out of his way. He strains himself to one of the basement walls and steps on some parts of the house to look around the vicinity.

Travis hobbles behind Ricky. "What do you see?"

"A shitload of dead people with missing body parts and another wave of them assholes getting up from the blast. They're gathering around Mikhael. Shit." Ricky jumps back down. "How we looking on ammo and guns?"

Alex inspects around. "Not good, I can't find my bag, and I only have my pistol."

"What about everyone else?" Ricky asks, addressing the others, who are doubtfully shaking their heads.

"Hold up," Ben says, full of hope. He kneels over a body that has a knife lodged in the back of its head. "Felicia killed him when he entered the basement a little while back. I can't believe he's still next to us and the blast didn't blow him away like it did everything else." Ben struggles for a second to remove the knife lodged in the man's skull and then searches the lifeless body. He finds the dead man's pistol. "He had an assault rifle, but I don't know what happened to it."

"Okay, that's two weapons to hold them off for a few shots, depending how big the magazines are," Travis says, sounding negative.

"Here." Ben tosses the gun at Ricky. "You're a better shot than me."

Ricky catches it. "Thanks." He looks at Alex. "Shall we?"

Alex confirms with a nod. The brothers find steady pieces of rubble to stand on next to the wall. They both point their pistols at the cartel coming at them with full force on the horizon, some in SUVs and others on foot.

Suddenly Travis's eyes widen. "Didn't you say there were two Predators?"

Alex flashes a foul facial expression and glances up to see a flying object zoom over their heads, releasing a huge missile. They witness the detonation and feel the breeze that comes with the shock wave. The explosion overtakes several of their adversaries as if it were a wave from the ocean taking victims in its undertow. Most of the militia are nowhere to be seen now.

Hearing the explosion brings much relief for those still in the basement. They show gratitude with fatigued smiles.

"Now's our chance. Everyone out of the basement. Pick up a fallen gun!" Ricky shouts. He pushes up and out of the basement, charging the enemy, while the ones who survived the explosion try to recover to their senses from the large blast.

Ben turns to Felicia before following the others. "Will you be fine?"

She nods, and Ben joins the charge, jumping out of what remains of the cellar.

Closer and closer they get to the enemy, picking up any rifle they can get their hands on. They sweep through the enemy, shooting any who are still alive.

"Look, it's Mikhael." James points.

"He's fleeing on foot!" Travis shouts.

"Cover me!" Alex yells, running after Mikhael.

"Forget that; he's mine!" Ricky cries out to Alex.

The two brothers dash ahead to catch Mikhael, spiriting nonstop for minutes. The brothers are led to the notorious mansion. They stand outside the front gate, monitoring for Mikhael.

"There!" Alex points to Mikhael's position, pushing the gate open. "He's entering the house."

Not to rush blindly and become victims of their own impatience, they stop at the entrance and carefully breach the house.

"Mikhael, you're not getting away from us. I'm going to kill you for what you did to my family," Ricky screams out, taking cover behind a wall and poking his head out slightly, scanning for Mikhael.

"Family?" Mikhael hollers. "That explains a lot."

Alex gains Ricky's attention with a tap on the shoulder. He performs tactical hand gestures that tell Ricky not to give away their location to Mikhael. Alex signals to Ricky that the voice was coming from upstairs.

Ricky gives a thumbs-up, and they both creep up the huge, elaborate staircase.

★★★

Mikhael kicks open his office doors, immediately opening the doorway to where the sisters are being held captive. He removes the girls from their shackles while pointing his pistol, threatening their lives just to be sure they won't try to flee. "I take it you're Mateo's familia?" he asks the girls rhetorically. "Well, Mateo, your family are now my new wives!" Mikhael speaks as if Mateo is next to him. He ties a rag around the girls' mouths so they can't say a word.

★★★

The brothers come to the studio where Mikhael is located. Alex peeps his head out to spot Mikhael tying his sheets together, making a rope. He ties it to a leg of his desk and tosses the tail end out the window. Mikhael feels the brothers breathing down his neck, spotting them by the door entrance. He fires a few warning shots at the doorway. "Get back or I'll kill them both." Mikhael points his gun at Stefani.

"You'd better not touch them, you piece of shit!" Ricky screams at Mikhael.

Stefani's eyes open wide, and she realizes her brother has come to their rescue.

"And what about my other family? My mother and other sister? Why did they have to die?" Alex asks Mikhael, taking cover on the other side of the door, facing Ricky.

As Mikhael pushes Kayla out the window, forcing her to climb down, he catches a twinkle of hope in her eye. He knows the end might come soon and feels that the girls know it too. "So these two are your little sisters huh? Well, the other two were probably not as pure and were going to be sold; they would have made me a little more money, too, until you guys messed all that up." Mikhael goes right behind Kayla, pointing his gun at Stefani and making her follow to the window, getting Kayla to cooperate fully with the fear that her sister will be harmed by Mikhael's gun. "But don't worry; these two will be taken care of. But your other family, like Mateo and everyone he loves, will die because of you two. And don't worry, this is not over; we will find you, and your end will come."

The two brothers look at each other, confused as to how he knows their grandfather.

Ricky peeps his head back into the room and sees they are not there. "Shit." Ricky runs to the open window with Alex behind him.

They both view the girls getting tossed into the back of Mikhael's SUV's rear hatch.

"Cover me," Alex says, climbing down the tied sheets.

Rick shoots toward Mikhael, rushing him into the car so gunfire won't be directed at Alex as he climbs down.

Mikhael starts his vehicle, watching Alex sprinting at him in the side mirror, taking aim. Mikhael stomps on the gas to take off. Unfortunately for Mikhael, Alex was given enough time to get off an accurate shot.

Alex fires several times, shooting through the back window, shattering the glass, and hitting Mikhael several times in the upper back.

The car comes to a halt. Alex jogs up to the truck with weapons drawn as Ricky climbs down from the window. Blood pouring profusely from his mouth, Mikhael spits up blood onto the windshield and steering wheel. He opens his door and tries to use what strength he has left to run. It's no use; he has too many bullet holes in his flesh. He falls onto his underbelly once he steps out, letting out a yipping sound.

Alex bolts to Mikhael's side, kicking the gun out of his reach.

Ricky hustles by his brother's side, pointing his pistol at Mikhael as well. He forcefully rolls Mikhael onto his back with a swift kick in the ribs. "Now tell us how you know Mateo." Ricky jams the barrel of his gun into Mikhael's forehead, slightly cracking his scalp.

A thin stream of blood trickles down his head into his vision, leaving Mikhael blind in one eye. He takes a second to gather his breath, wheezing from his lungs filling with blood. "Whoever Mateo is to you, he is the one who sent me these girls."

Alex looks at Ricky in confusion. "No. Grandpa wouldn't do that."

"Don't you lie!" Ricky whips his pistol across Mikhael's face, causing severe damage to his teeth.

Numb and in shock from the loss of blood, Mikhael barely feels the impact and continues to speak after pushing a tooth out with his tongue. "Why would I lie? I'm dying, and you two are going to kill me. He owed me, and I told him to get me American girls or I'd kill his entire family."

"Holy Crist. Why? *Augh!*" Ricky walks away, frustrated, and gathers his thoughts.

"This is all Grandpa's doing? We have to confront him!" Alex says to Ricky.

"You're right, but first this piece of shit." Ricky pins his gun back on Mikhael, placing the cold steel of the barrel on his throat. You killed my mom and my sister Brittany. This is for them."

Alex places his gun to Mikhael's neck as well and faces Ricky with a nod. Mikhael closes his eyes, and the brothers simultaneously pull their triggers. The two stand to watch Mikhael struggle for air, thrashing furiously like a worm that has just been torn in half. The brothers don't move an inch, with rage-filled eyes. Mikhael's life eventually comes to an end with the two brothers hovering in his sight until his vision blurs to black.

CHAPTER 19

THEIR EYES FILLED WITH FURY and the news of betrayal, Ricky and his brother rush over to the girls. The back hatch swings open. The girls cradle each other, crying in fear of the unknown and hoping their comfort is enough to settle the eerie suspense.

The brothers wipe the tears away, and the pressure to overcome the impossible lifts off their shoulders. Their long journey finally is coming to an end.

The girls lift their chins and block out the sunlight with their hands to gaze upon their brothers standing there with smiles on their faces. They began to slowly come to their senses and greet their heroes with a burst of relief. Alex and Ricky hug their sisters, raise them out of the rear of the SUV, place them ever so lightly onto the soil the truck has stalled on. The two girls have had their senses dulled for so long that the feeling of their bare feet touching earth brings new light to their eyes.

As she lies in his arms, Alex brushes back Stefani's hair softly. "It's okay, it's okay. We are here."

Kayla looks up at Ricky while hugging him. "Did you find Mom and Brittany?"

Ricky holds Kayla tighter with endearment. "They didn't make it."

Stefani hears Ricky. "What? No, no. Why!" Stefani tries to drop to the ground from the pain her sorrow creates, but she is pulled close to Alex yet again.

"No, we weren't fast enough. I'm sorry." Alex tightens his hug on Stefani.

Kayla stops hugging Ricky, softly brushing him off. "I need a moment."

"Yeah." Ricky lets go of her with sympathy.

Stefani moves aside Alex gently. "I'll be fine." She covers her eyes because of the stress the news has brought and walks over to Kayla.

Kayla wraps her arms around Stefani and holds her sister. Kayla whispers in her ear, "We will be okay; our brothers will take care of us. We will be fine."

Stefani's disbelief leaves her arms limp, but the hug her sister brings gives her enough strength to shake off the fantasy of her mother and older sister being alive. She finally comes to grasp reality and inhales deeply, embracing her sister. Seconds later, Stefani concludes her clasp and looks at her brothers. "What did you do with that bad guy?" she looks around. "Is he still here?"

Ricky points to the other side of the car. "We killed him. He's over there."

"Good," Kayla says angrily.

Stefani runs around the car. Alex and Ricky glance at each other, puzzled at Stefani's actions. The three follow behind her to witness what she is up to.

"What are you—" Alex stops in midsentence upon witnessing what Stefani is doing.

Ricky picks Stefani up and pulls her away from the corpse, stopping her from kicking the lifeless figure repeatedly in the side of the head.

"Ahh!" Stefani screams toward Mikhael's remains. "Put me down. He deserves more punishment!"

"Stop, Stefani," Ricky scolds her. "He's dead. There's nothing more we can do to harm him."

Tears drip down from Stefani's eyes. "I know, but he killed Mom and Brittany and took us and chained us up and … and …"

"It's okay, Stefani." Kayla says, cradling her. "He got what he deserved."

"He didn't die peacefully; we can tell you that." Alex points to a huge amount of blood dripping from his throat.

"I just wish I could have seen it," Stefani begs, filled with mixed emotions.

"You've been through enough," Alex says. "You both have, and we didn't want you two to see any more."

Kayla's eye catches the smoke in the air in the far distance. She looks beyond the property to behold the destruction in the distance. "So you two did all that?"

"Kind of," Ricky answers.

"We had help from friends," Alex adds.

"Who?" Stefani asks.

"Them." Ricky points to Travis, James, and Ben, who are carrying Felicia up the mansion's long driveway.

"And a friend far away from here. He's on a ship," Alex adds. "If not for his sacrifice, this wouldn't have been possible."

"Yeah, I should have known they would have helped," Stefani says of Ben and James, already knowing them.

"You know they are like my right hand." Ricky raises his arms up in the air as if to hug them from a distance while walking toward the group with his sisters and brother following.

Kayla shows incertitude. "Who is Ben carrying, and why?"

"Her name is Felicia, and she helped us a lot. If not for her, we wouldn't be here. She provided a van for us all. We met her a little while back. After she listened to our story, she volunteered to help us." Alex leaves out the fact that they kidnapped her, thinking it unnecessary at the moment. He lifts his chin at the group with pride. "And the reason she is being carried by Ben, I think, is because she might have broken her ankle in the blasts I'm sure you heard in the distance."

"Oh, that sucks." Kayla looks at the group, noticing their torn attire and how they carry themselves, appearing exhausted from their journey. She understands what they must have been through as they come closer. "I appreciate you all helping us," she mentions to the others as the two groups eventually make it to one another.

"Yeah, me too," Stefani adds to Kayla's appreciation.

"De nada," Felicia comments while still being assisted by Ben. Her arm is over his shoulder as she limps.

Knowing the situation is extremely sensitive, Ben utters only a simple acknowledgment. "Hey, Kayla. Hey, Stefani."

"Are you two okay?" James asks.

Staying stoic, the girls show only slight gratitude by their facial expressions and small nods.

"So these are your sisters." Travis introduces himself and shakes Kayla and Stefani's hands. "Pleasure to meet you two; my name is Travis. I'm Alex's other brother from the military. Sorry we took so long to get you."

"We are fine now, so don't mention it," Stefani says, thinking with displeasure of her situation.

Travis perceives the pain they've been through, which they show through their body language. He does not press the matter.

"I don't know about you, but when we entered that guy's room, I saw he had a safe up there, probably full of all types of valuable crap." Ricky moves forward, approaching the mansion. "Let's go check it out."

The others follow Ricky, with Felicia still riding along on Ben, stepping over and around the dead corpse that was once Mikhael. One of his hands is still grasping his neck from trying to stop the blood from pouring out. His eyes are lifeless and tinted gray.

They enter the room to see Ricky already going through the safe. "I guess he wanted to get some stuff out but ran out of time when he noticed we were so close behind him. He even forgot to shut the door." Ricky moves out of the way to let the others scrutinize. "Look, money." Ricky has a huge grin on his face.

Everyone's eyes widen and their mouths drop at what they see.

"There has to be a few million here," Ben says aloud as he peruses the mound of cash.

"I wouldn't know; it's all in pesos," Ricky replies.

"Hey, Felicia." James skips up to the safe, leans over the top, and peeps his head inside. "How much American money you think is here?"

Felicia slowly limps to the safe, softly walking on her foot. She does a double-take, not believing that her first glimpse was correct. She kneels to better count how many stacks there are and how much is in one bundle. "Cuatro millones de pesos." She stands with excitement. "Cuatro millones de pesos!" she repeats with a small jump her happiness generates, neglecting the pain of her foot. "Ey!" she yells out when she lands. The pain gives her a quick slap back to the severity of her injury.

Ben catches her before she falls. "Are you okay? I guess that's a lot." He chuckles, making eye contact with the object of his infatuation. He looks at the others. "How much would you say that is, in English?"

James scratches the side of his head. "Well, *cuatro* sounds familiar."

"Cuatro is four, you ass. It's so simple. Something you should have learned in grade school," Alex says.

"Oh, that, right." James laughs as the simple Spanish word goes over his head. "So what's the other part then?"

"Four million pesos." Kayla rolls her eyes. "It sounds just like English. So I guess she can't speak English." She shakes her head. "How did you guys manage to speak to each other?"

James answers Kayla. "Well, we had an app on my phone, but it got destroyed."

"So what is that in American money? Three million in American dollars?" Travis estimates.

Alex ponders. "Yeah, that sounds correct, give or take."

"Now I guess we split it." Ricky points to Felicia. "Split this into eight." Ricky turns to the group. "Does that sound fair to everyone? I don't want to hear no crying afterward." Ricky eyeballs everyone to validate that no one disagrees with the idea of the way he suggests the money should be split. "'Ight, go ahead." Ricky guides Felicia to divide the money with arm gestures.

"Que?" Felicia asks.

"Oh yeah, she doesn't speak English or understand that well," Ricky says, remembering. "Shoot."

Kayla interrupts Ricky to translate for Felicia. "Dividir el dinero en ocho."

Felicia acknowledges Kayla and starts to count.

Amazed by her Spanish, Alex asks his sister, "When did you learn Spanish, Kayla?"

"She learned last year in her Spanish class," Stefani answers for Kayla.

"Yeah, they're making everyone take a foreign class and pass in order to graduate," Kayla says scornfully.

"I guess being part of the military makes me miss a lot of your guys' lives." Alex bows his head with grief.

"I'll go find us some bags." James wanders off.

Ben follows. "I'll help."

"Hecho." Felicia stands and admires her work. She has eight stacks of pesos in front of her.

"So what's that?" Alex asks as he tries to do the math. "Four million divided by eight?"

"I found this inside the desk." Stefani holds up an object to her brothers, Felicia, Travis, and her sister. "A calculator." Stefani enters the number. "Four million divided by eight, you said?"

"Yeah," Alex confirms, waiting patiently for the answer.

"Wow, we all get five hundred thousand dollars." Stefani reads off.

"What's that in America?" Ricky frowns in frustration at his inability to convert the value of pesos and US dollars.

"I would say around ... three hundred thousand," Travis answers.

"Now the question is, How will we convert this money to US dollars and get back home?" Ricky asks aloud.

"We can worry about converting the money some other time. But since we are related to Kayla and Stefani, we have to sneak back into America. I figure the girls can go home by going to an American embassy and telling them I saved them by killing Mikhael and was the only one responsible for this destruction."

"What? Forget that!" Ricky says, looking concerned.

"Let me finish." Alex quickly stops Ricky from assuming the worst. He knows Ricky won't want to listen and will want to take the blame as well, not letting Alex take on all of the guilt. "Since I'm the only one that has any chance to get a few years, and I'm the only one that the government will believe could have done this devastation alone, I'll go, and while I'm getting interrogated, I'll tell them it was only me. The girls will say the same thing; I'm the only one they saw that helped them escape."

"I hate that idea ... but I guess you're right," Ricky replies.

Alex considers Felicia's knowledge and gains his sister's attention to get her to translate. "Hey Kayla, ask Felicia if she knows any coyotes."

"Coyotes?" Kayla wonders about the animal but compiles anyway. "Como sabes ... coyotes?" she asks Felicia.

Felicia considers the question and concludes that the term "coyote" refers to a smuggler. "Mi primo."

"Your cousin? That's cool," Ricky says.

"How much money? Dinero?" Alex asks Felicia.

"Nada." She shakes her head. "Después de que yo le digo que mataste Mikhael."

"What did she say, Kayla?" Alex asks.

"She said he won't charge anything because you killed Mikhael."

"Hell yeah," James says, walking in with Ben, their hands full of duffel bags, snacks, drinks, and more weapons.

"You guys aren't coming," Ricky states.

"Why not?" Ben tosses everyone a bag of chips, a drink, and a duffel bag. "Here."

"Thanks." Stefani snatches the bag of chips out of the air and eats viciously. "I was so hungry."

"Me too," Kayla adds with a mouth full of chips.

"You are not going, because you didn't do anything wrong and just misplaced your passport and ID." Ricky says, insisting on the imaginary situation between James and Ben. "You will be going to the embassy with Kayla and Stefani—not together though. Just ask to be sent back home. You guys also don't know Kayla or Stefani. They do this part alone."

Ben analyzes Ricky's plan. "Oh, that sucks. And I take it you're not going because you're related to your sisters and they would put two and two together?"

"Yeah, so I have to sneak back to the US with Felicia's help," Ricky replies. "Alex is the only one wanted, and since he is part of the military, they probably won't make his sentence as long. So he's going to take the whole rap."

"What the hell, man?" James comments.

Travis agrees with Alex. "It's the only way if we don't want to get caught."

"Man, whatever," Ben says.

"What about you, Travis?" Alex asks, sounding concerned.

"My wife, she is still with all my stuff at Tampico, so I'll be fine. I just need one of you guys to take some of my money," Travis says as he stuffs his bag.

Ricky joins Travis in stuffing his bag with the money. "Yeah, Alex and I will take the money, and we will split it again when we meet up in Flint."

"Felicia is the lucky one; she can just keep the money and not worry about transferring it," James says.

"Yeah, she is somewhat lucky," Travis agrees, his tone indicating his recognition of her having endured a lot.

Ricky and Alex take the bags of money and head downstairs to the garage.

"I'm sure he has more than that one truck that Alex shot down, judging by that garage connected to this place." Ricky searches the lower floor door by door, trying to find his way to the garage. In no time, he finds the entrance. "Yup, I was right." Ricky discovers a switch by the doorframe and clicks it. Light after light comes on, revealing remarkable vehicles. He clicks a button directly next to the switch, assuming and establishing it is the button to open the garage doors.

The rest enter the garage to look at five beautiful, expensive vehicles, including a foreign sports car and two SUVs. One of the SUVs appears ready to be painted and has been modernized with all types of flashy electronics; the other resembles an untouched off-road lifted Jeep.

"Now which one do you want, Felicia? You're the only one who will be able to keep it. But unfortunately, you have to pick one that will fit us all, unlike that sports car over there." Alex points and asks his sister to translate.

She steps forward and then glances back to the others for assurance. "Cualquier coche que quiero?" She is hesitant to accept this blessing. She wanders around limping, checking out each treasure, finally deciding to hop inside the brand-new SUV that's teched out, but the keys are nowhere to be found. Everyone participates to help locate the keys by scanning all around.

"Found them!" Kayla yanks out the keys from under the driver's-side seat and tosses them to Felicia. "Here, you forgot to look in the most obvious spot."

Stefani jumps inside the back of the SUV and buckles up. "Now let's get out of this place."

Felicia leans to Alex as he positions himself next to her in the front passenger seat. "A donde?" she asks.

"We will go to the closest American embassy," Ricky says, sitting directly behind Felicia.

"American embassy?" She thinks where she's at while starting the vehicle, bracing herself to use her good foot. "No se donde esta."

"She doesn't know where that is," Kayla says.

"Oh shoot, now what?" James says, aggravated.

"What's that?" Ben points to a built-in GPS directly under the car's radio. He sits between Ricky and Stefani.

"Hell yeah, that's a GPS!" Travis hollers with joy from the far back with James.

Alex pushes the touch screen global positioning system symbols that he thinks might activate the device. "Now let's see if I can … Got it. The closest embassy is in Nuevo Laredo. Wherever that is, and it looks like it will take us. Ugh."

"What?" Ben asks impatiently.

"Seven hours away!" Ricky reads. "Better make myself comfortable."

Alex clicks the start button. "Now routing," the GPS speaks aloud

"Hmm, the GPS is in English. How weird," Travis states.

"Hey, we're in luck. It's directly next to the border, so we won't need your primo, Felicia." Alex turns to Felicia as she puts the car in drive to move out of the open garage door. "Kayla, tell her what I said to you."

"Entiendo," Felicia answers before Kayla can translate.

"She understood you," Kayla notifies her brother.

"Oh, okay. Another good thing is that it's next to our uncle and cousin Gilbert's hometown—Laredo, Texas," Alex adds.

"Hell yeah, we can ask him for help crossing the border to make it easier on us," Ricky says.

"Hey Felicia, are you okay to drive the whole time?" Ben asks, sounding concerned.

"Of course not," Ricky answers for Felicia. "We will do what we did to get here. Take turns."

"So the same routine with who comes next?" Travis asks.

"Sounds good; let's do that," Alex answers. "Well, since I'm not up to drive for a while, I'm getting some rest." He puts his seat in a reclined position. "Still got room, Stefani?"

"Yeah, I'm okay," Stefani answers, looking out the window while trying to organize her thoughts.

"Yeah, that sounds like a good idea," James agrees, lightly leaning his head on the window. He embraces the vibration, which soothes his chaotic alert state, releasing him into a relaxed desire.

Alex's heart is full of grief as he studies his youngest sibling continuously staring out the window. He is aware his two sisters will need intense help to get over this tragic incident. He lays his head back, closing his eyes, aware that his sisters are in good hands. Knowing this lets him obtain some well-deserved rest.

When the conversations spread from a few to none, Ricky is sulking, his eyes burning with rage. Mixed emotions overcome his demeanor. Someone whom he had high respect for, his grandfather Mateo, will soon be confronted.

CHAPTER 20

"HEY, WAKE UP." STEFANI MOVES Alex's shoulder from behind his seat.

Alex barely opens his eyes to look around. "My turn to drive already?"

"No, silly," Stefani answers.

"We are a few blocks from the embassy, in the parking lot of some motel," James says to Alex.

"I can't believe I slept that whole time. How come no one woke me?" Alex shakes his head to snap out of his tired state of mind.

"Well, technically it is your turn to drive," Travis says, "but we split the car ride into two-hour shifts. Ben, James, and I weren't that tired, so we just decided to drive the whole time and let everyone else sleep."

"Sounds good to me," Ricky replies as he wakes with a stretch.

"I figure I'll park here so we all can have a quick shower." Ben plugs his nose with a smile. "We all smell. No offense."

"Pagaré. I pay," Felicia says, climbing over Ben first to exit. After a quick stretch, she walks inside the main office, evaluating the building's status as a single-story cliché. It is run-down and in need of routine repairs.

"So you guys do anything freaky yet?" Ricky asks Ben.

"What do you mean? We had no time. But I was thinking maybe I'll kiss her before I go to the embassy." Ben blushes with a bright smile.

In no time at all, Felicia comes out with a key in her hand and waves the group to follow. "Sígueme."

The group leaves the truck and meets with Felicia. They search for their number, passing by all the other rooms and finally reaching their door.

A few hours go by, and everyone is out of the shower, clean, and refreshed, although still wearing the same clothes.

Felicia returns the key to the front desk, leaving the woman who is standing behind the desk with a confused look due to their not needing the room for the night stay.

"I'll drive," Alex says while reentering the SUV. He searches in between the seats and around the dashboard. "Where are the keys at?"

"I still got 'em." James pulls the keys outside of his pocket. "Here." He hands them over to Alex.

Soon they find themselves back on the road, coming closer to the embassy.

When they finally make it, Alex does a quick pass, locating all cameras. He parks next to the curb outside the line of sight of any surveillance.

"James, Ben—get out," Ricky orders. "You will be the first to go. Remember: you don't know the girls, and you just lost your passports and ID."

"Make sure you take enough money to cover any charges, like a taxi and an airport ticket afterward to fly back to Flint," Alex reminds them.

"Oh yeah, good looking out." Ben digs through his bag. "Oh, and before I go." Ben leans into Felicia and kisses her.

She kisses him back for several seconds. The intimacy between them everyone sensed finally comes through.

"Ugh. Right next to me?" Stefani rolls her eyes. "How disgusting."

"I know you don't know English, but maybe you can teach me Spanish or I could teach you English, and we can go somewhere with this. You and your kids could come and visit … Shoot, I don't know." Ben starts to look nervous.

Felicia seeks a piece of paper and something to write with. She writes down her home phone number and hands it to Ben. They both smile widely. With a huge smile still on his face, Ben does the Rude Boys gang handshake with Ricky.

James follows and shakes Ricky's hand as well. The two part ways with the others without saying more than what is needed. Good-byes are not a strong suit with anyone here, especially after their recent exploit.

The girls give hugs to James and Ben to give them credit for their heroism once more.

"See ya." Ricky waves to the girls as they walk toward the embassy.

After a few seconds of silence, and after Ben and James are out of view, Ricky, Alex, Stefani, and Kayla hug one another. The two girls tag-team Felicia and hug her as well.

"Remember: only I was the one who took care of you and saved you," Alex reminds them.

The girls nod with understanding. They get out of the car and hold each other's hands, walking slowly to the embassy with the thought of Alex being the only one who saved them.

They enter the embassy and walk up to the first person they see—a well-groomed woman behind a desk on the phone.

"My name is Kayla, and this is my sister, Stefani. We were captured by a man named Mikhael Trevijano Morales."

The woman ends her phone call and shows much shock at the name Kayla just mentioned.

"Mikhael Trevijano Morales is dead now; my brother killed him and dropped us off here." Stefani adds.

The woman stands up in shock. Her eyes are attracted to scenes of devastation on the television in the corner of the office. The footage shows an eagle's-eye view from a hovering helicopter over Saltillo. "Follow me." She quickly starts to walk toward a set of elevators, pulling the youngest of the sisters by her hand.

★★★

Back with the others, Alex sighs at the new challenge and turns to his brother. "Now let's go to the edge of the city and get past this border patrol." Alex pulls the gear stick into drive and rides off.

The border comes into the line of view faster than anticipated. They do a few passes to watch the portal and check where they are stationed. Only a few are located along the fence.

Ricky notices that the fence has cameras along the border as well, making the matter more complicated. "I don't see a way in. It's all monitored by cameras. And the guards don't look to be the friendliest. They kinda seem athletic."

"Yeah, I bet they run a lot. We are going to need a distraction. After this you can finally take Travis home." Alex looks to Felicia. "But first we are going to need to buy some masks. We don't need our faces to be seen on camera."

A few hours later, after they finally have the plan together, they say their farewells.

The moon brightens the sky, and Felicia slowly limps to the fence following the border between the two countries. She shakes the cage railing furiously and tries to run along the side of the barrier as fast as her ankle will allow her, shouting as if she were a rabid feral beast.

"Ugh, another drunken Mexican trying to fuck with us. This happens every night," a border patrol officer says to his fellow coworkers playing a game of cards. "So who's going to stop this one?" He looks around to see no volunteers. "Fine, I will." He bows his head to their inside rule—first to see, first to act. He picks his belt up from his waist, adjusting his uniform. He walks to the fence and stops inches away from Felicia. "Ma'am, ma'am!" he yells.

Felicia stops running, and acts so crazy to look at the officer. "Que?"

"You need to stop." The border patrol officer puts one hand on his gun and points to her to back away.

She glances behind the man and watches the brothers sneak beside the building where the border patrol workers are located.

Too distracted by Felicia being mad, none of the border patrol workers look around or to the cameras.

Felicia shrugs her shoulders and walks away from the fence once she is sure the brothers are out of sight.

"Thank God, this one was easy," the border patrol officer tells himself.

★★★

Alex stops a few miles away in the pitch dark, out of the spotlight of the border patrol. He turns back to view the lights in the distance, carrying a few bags full of money and guns. "Thank you, Felicia. I'm sorry for all we put you through. I hope the money and vehicle were enough," he says out loud.

"We'll probably see her soon since Ben and her have a thing now," Ricky says, walking past Alex as he heads closer to the next town nonchalantly. "No need to get into your emotions."

"Yeah, you're right," Alex agrees. "So how do you feel about them as a couple?"

"It's straight, I guess. Kind of weird, but cool," Ricky answers.

"Yeah, she's a lot older than him, but I guess that's good for him," Alex replies.

An hour into walking through town using the shadows as cover, they arrive outside of their cousin Gilbert's house. They lie in bushes just outside of the house, using the shadows as cover to go over what they will say and what they will leave out. They look upon a small trailer home on a lot with little to no yard. A short driveway leads to an aluminum shed attached to the side of the house.

When the coast is clear, they move in quickly. Alex pushes the doorbell, and a ring echoes throughout the house. A man wearing gym shorts, house shoes, and a tank top answers. His stomach shows from consuming one too many beers in the last few years, and he seems to have just been woken up. His hair is messy and long. If not for being so wavy, it would reach down to his shoulders. He stands slightly taller than the brothers.

Gilbert's eyes widen and he snaps out of tiredness when he sees who it is. "Holy crap! What are you guys doing here? You two look like you've been through hell."

Ricky, being the up-front and direct one of the brothers, talks first. "I'm sorry to tell you this but we are in a hurry and need your help."

"Sure, sure, anything for family. Come in." He backs up to let the two brothers in.

Alex and Ricky make their way inside the house. It appears as if a bachelor has lived there for years. Clothes have been tossed on lamps, and empty pizza boxes are stacked next to the garbage in the kitchen. Dishes fill the sink. They have been waiting to be cleaned for weeks.

Alex stops studying the house and cuts to the chase. "Well, we didn't want to get you involved, but we came across some problems, and we need a car." Alex drops one of his bags and pulls out a stack of money to show his cousin Gilbert. "Got any idea who will sell us a car in pesos?"

"Wow! How much is that?" Gilbert is surprised at the amount of money shown to him. "And what are you doing with all that money?"

Ricky places his hand on his cousin's shoulder. "We don't want to get you more involved than you already are. But it's about thirty thousand pesos."

"Well, you can take my car for that much; it runs really well." Gilbert starts to turn around and head for his room. "Let me just get the title."

Ricky stops him from proceeding any father then a few steps. "No need. Just call it in tomorrow as stolen. And don't worry about us getting caught. We will deal with the car; I know how."

"Okay, great." He takes the money from Alex with a huge grin, counting the money.

Ricky thinks to himself about his grandfather and whether Mikhael was telling the truth. He wants to find out a little more about their grandfather's past and whether it intertwines with Mikhael. Knowing their grandfather is full of stories, the two brothers don't really know what is real and what is fake. Ricky figures now is a good time to retrieve some information from their grandfather's side of the family and maybe have some stories become clearer. "So do you know the story of how our grandfather Mateo came to America?" Ricky asks, knowing that his grandfather was close to Gilbert's grandfather.

Though he does not understand why this question came so abruptly, Gilbert cooperates. "Yeah, my grandpa told me a few years back. Let me see, where should I start …"

CHAPTER 21

Fifty years prior, San Luis Potosi, Mexico

MATEO SHIELDS THE SUN FROM hitting his eyes with his hand. He wipes the sleep away and sits up from slumber. He has no alarm clock, so he counts on the sun to wake him up. He leaves his bedside to put his clothes on. Ready for the day, he walks out of his bedroom. His mother is already up and has made a full breakfast for his sister and him.

"Mateo, can you wake your *hermana por favor?*" his mother asks as she sets the table.

"Si madre." Mateo graciously walks into the room across from him to notice that his sister has not woken yet and is sleeping on her side, facing the wall. Mateo kneels next to her and with a loving voice says, "Maria, mi lovely hermana of mine, it's time to wake up. *Madre* has made breakfast."

Maria rolls over with her eyes still closed, facing her brother. "Okay."

Knowing his sister is stubborn and will not get out of bed that easily he starts to ask simple questions. "So what are you dreaming of?"

Maria shrugs her shoulders with her eyes still closed.

"So how did you sleep? You look very comfortable," Mateo says.

Finally Maria answers, but her eyes are still closed. "I did, I slept very good. I dreamed of *Papi.*" Her green eyes open and sparkle. "He said he loves us all; we were in a field of flowers, and he was sitting on his tombstone. We were having the best conversation."

Mateo smiles. "Sounds beautiful. One day the vaccine for tuberculosis will make it here and no one else will die." He begins to walk out of her room. He stops by the doorway and glimpses over his shoulder. "Now get up, hermana; mama is waiting." Mateo smiles and walks out of the room.

Later, after everybody is full and all the food is gone, everyone is cleaned up and ready for the day. Oración, Maria and Mateo's mother, is cleaning the dishes in a large bowl of water and soap suds. "Are you off?"

"Yes, Mother, I'm going to work." Mateo walks up to his mother and kisses her cheek. Oración hands him his lunch his sister packed for him.

As Mateo proceeds out the door, his sister stops him with a hug. "Have a good day, *hermano*."

Delighted from the squeeze, he looks upon his sister. "Thank you for my lunch, and good luck on your test today at school." After the love is shown, Mateo continues out of his house and proceeds to the closest bus stop.

★★★

"What a good son, going to work elsewhere, making a little extra money than what he would make here. He knows the store was his father's dream, so he does what he can to keep it open. He helps more than he knows, paying the bills when the store I look after can't, while his sister goes to school. I'm so proud." Oración looks at her daughter with a smile. "You know, if not for your brother, we wouldn't be able to keep the store running and keep our house."

Maria smiles back at her mother. "I'm sure it's easier to keep up with now since Papi made it a part of the house."

"Yes, but nevertheless, your brother helps a tremendous amount." Oración pauses. "He has so much spirit, like his padre." Oración looks at the clock on the wall. "Look at the time; we've got to send you on your way."

Maria picks up her backpack while Oración opens up the door. Maria pecks her mother on the cheek, leaving the house and making her way down the street.

Oración waves, yelling out, "Bye, have a beautiful day, hija!" She shuts the door behind her with a full heart, as she does every day. She enters her room and opens a door that is located on the back wall of the bedroom. When she opens it, the smell of various spices and foods rush her senses as a grocery store stockroom would. The room is full of products she sells; cardboard boxes are stacked to the ceiling. An opening that is enclosed by a beaded curtain beams light inside. She pushes back the beads and turns on the lights of the store. With it being so small, it just takes a few more steps to flip over a sign, changing it from "closed" to "open." She unlocks the door to begin the day. She then finds her way back to where the lights are and stands behind the cash register.

Customers come, and hours go. Soon Maria comes back from school. She enters the store door, and her mom greets her with much enthusiasm. "Hija, do you have any homework?"

"No, Mama, I'll help you with the store once I eat something and put away my stuff."

"Gracias, hija."

Maria peeks around the store.

Oración notices. "Looking for Mateo?"

Maria nods. "Yeah, where is he?"

"I'm not sure." Oración looks somewhat concerned. "He did say earlier this week he might have some overtime."

"Oh, okay." Maria hears the store's door being opened by a customer. "Well, I'll be back; I'll go warm up some of yesterday's *sopa*." She licks her lips.

Oración seems concerned but acknowledges her daughter. "Okay, hija." Maria moves aside the beads behind Oración while the customers who just entered step up to Oración. "Can I help you three?"

A tall, thin man standing to the right of their group pushes off a counter advertisement item. "Don't play, *pendeja!* You know why we are here."

The man in the middle cuts off the one already speaking, "Now just give us the money to protect you, and we will be on our way."

Oración shows a tremendous amount of fear. "I don't know why I need protection; this city is too small, and all we have to fear here are you thugs."

The third man, who has yet to speak, finally makes a move. He pulls out a small revolver from his jeans and looks at it while saying,

"Well, since we are the only ones in this run-down small shit city to have a gun, you'd better listen." He slowly points it at Oración. "Now pay up, *puta*."

Oración stares at a blank wall out of terror. "Mi hijo has the money; he gets paid today. He's just running behind schedule. I promise I'll have the money."

The three men look at one other. The firearm holder speaks for the group to Oración. "Well, we can't have this happen again, but we will let you go this time. We expect the money tomorrow." The three men rotate and face the exit. As they exit the door, the one who seems to be in charge, the man holding the weapon, smirks over his shoulder at Oración. "Oh, yeah, that's right. We can't let you go without a punishment." He proceeds to walk out, nodding to the other two. They turn around, face Oración, and sprint toward her.

"Please, please!" Oración yells out.

Hours later, Mateo opens the store's door with a huge smile while calling out for his mother. "Mama, guess what? You will never expect—" Mateo stops midsentence upon noticing Oración's face and how her eyes are swollen, filled with tears, as his baby sister comforts her. "Madre? Wh-what happened?"

Too ashamed of her face, she buries her head into her daughter's arms. "You know those guys who mama claimed to be family who come in once a month?" Maria looks deep into Mateo's eyes. "Well, they weren't. They are part of a gang they made up, and they come to stores like this to offer protection from them. That sounds pretty stupid, huh?"

Mateo hesitantly stumbles to his mother's side and places his hand on her back. "Mama, I'm sorry. I know you were asking about the money, but I never knew—"

Maria interrupts Mateo. "If it wasn't for me overhearing the noise of them beating mama and coming out here with a bat, they would still be beating her." Maria puts on a face of disgust. "And you know how policía is limited here in our small town. I don't know what to do; they told mama they will be back to collect and this is just a warning."

Mateo glances down at his mother and sister with a worried expression. He panics, and adrenaline takes over his thinking process.

He staggers out of the store and decides to hunt down these men. "Mijo! Don't do anything foolish!" his mother cries out as he pushes the store's door open with force. Filled with rage, he ignores his mother.

Living in such a small town and thinking the assailants were family, he knows just where they hang out: in an ally just outside of town next to two condemned buildings—a place where only the homeless stay.

Without any issues, he finds the men in a matter of minutes. As he strides up to the three, he overhears how proud they are of having beaten up such a helpless woman. They are around a car that seems to have caught fire days before. The head goon kneels on the hood while the other two listen.

"Tu!" Mateo yells out pointing at the three men. "Are you the ones who did the beating to that woman in the store?"

The three look at one another and laugh out loud. The leader speaks. "Yeah, what's it to you? What are you going to do about it, *cono*?" He looks at his two friends, smug and full of reassurance.

Mateo stutters and grasps the thought of what he just got himself into. "Yo-you better not come near that store o-or any other store again!"

The three glance at each other, sensing little to no threat. The tall, thin thug leans over to the others. "Let's waste this fool."

Mateo steps back out of fear, gulps, and takes two steps forward. "One at a time." He raises his fists.

"Que?" The main vandal says.

Mateo answers, "I'll take you on, but one at a time."

"Ha! You think you can take us on one at a time?" He laughs as he hands his pistol off. "Take this. I don't need help to beat you down."

Mateo and the man square up to fight. This being Mateo's first fight, he thinks of his father and how he taught him how to hold his fists when he was a child.

Mateo's opponent connects with the first swing. It takes a few more hits to the face before Mateo is knocked into reality and begins to fight back. His adrenaline finally kicks in. Having worked in construction and done lifting heavy most of his life, Mateo has no idea what strength he has. He closes his eyes and swings with all of his might. To his surprise, he connects with the man's face. Mateo watches as he falls onto his butt.

The guy's friends start to laugh. On the dusty ground, he glares at the others making fun of him. Embarrassed, he takes out a switchblade from his shoe and stands up, pointing it at Mateo. "You shouldn't have done that. Now I'll kill you."

Mateo raises his hands in the air in the perfect stance to take a knife out of his opponent's hand. Without knowing this, he begs, "Please, I don't want any trouble; I just want you guys to leave this town alone."

"Die!" The man lunges at Mateo

Mateo unconsciously stops the knife from entering his stomach, catching the wrist of his adversary inches from his belly. Mateo thinks quickly. With all his might, he kicks the man's knee inward, hearing a bone-breaking crunch that reverberates throughout the area. The injury forces Mateo's foe to cling to Mateo. The two fall, with Mateo on his back and the other man on top. Mateo rolls the man off of him. He notices that the blade is lodged deep in the man's abdomen when he grunts from the pain.

The other two, having witnessed their friend get stabbed, are briefly in a state of shock. Mateo knows he must react quickly. It is his life or theirs. He pulls out the blade, leaving a small trail of blood over the victim's shirt. The man's pained screams echo throughout the alley. Mateo spirits at the man who holds the gun. Before it can be pointed, Mateo plunges the knife into his neck.

Gasping for air, the man falls to his knees, dropping the gun. He struggles to remove the knife from his neck, trying to push Mateo away. The amount of blood loss keeps his strength low.

As Mateo struggles to remove the knife, he is struck with a bat on the side of his neck. The blow gives Mateo the twitch he would have for the rest of his life. He falls to the ground, going in and out of consciousness. He feels pain in his leg when the man hits him once more with the bat.

The man steps over Mateo with his weapon raised upward behind his head, aiming for Mateo's face. His full amount of strength will be behind this swing, and there is a high chance Mateo will not survive the blow. Barely conscious and his movements limited from the first strike to his neck, Mateo gazes around for help. He spots the gun inches from his hand. As the bat comes down, Mateo grasps for the gun. He closes his eyes once the gun is in his hand, pulling the trigger as fast as his finger will let him, emptying the chamber. Mateo, uninjured, opens his eyes to witness the man backing up, grasping at the holes that were just placed inside him as he slowly falls to the pavement. Knowing the threat is over, Mateo's vision turns black.

Mateo wakes in his bed with a huge headache and an excessive amount of pain in his left knee and neck. His mother is next to him. "Mama? What … How did I get here?"

"No matter, Mijo; you're safe, and those men won't be bothering us again, thanks to you." She brushes back his hair, comforting him.

Mateo grins at his mother's still swollen face. "Why didn't you tell me about them? I would have come home faster; I would have found a different way of dealing with them a long time ago."

Oración looks away in shame. "Your father dealt with them; I didn't know how to handle it."

Mateo takes a deep breath in. "Well, I guess they're gone now."

Oración looks at Mateo with distress. "No, when our neighbors got there to get you, only two were dead. One got away, and what your father told me about them is not good. I guess they are a small branch from a bigger gang in Saltillo. The man who carried the gun, the one who didn't die, is the *sobrino* of some big shot." Oración watches Mateo's face become overwhelmed with worry. "Did you tell them you were my son?"

"No, Mama, I just told them to leave the city."

Oración places her hand on his forearm with relief. "Then there's hope." She smiles. "Pack your things and take your father's car. It still runs. I'll make a few calls, and I can get you out of Mexico and into America. You can stay with your Tio. your papa's *armono.* He lives in Laredo, Texas."

"Thanks, Mama." Mateo rises out of bed and begins to pack his things with the help of his sister and mother. Once Mateo is all packed, he abruptly stops by the door.

Maria seems concerned. "Hermano?"

Mateo takes a second to respond. "It's just that I have to tell you both why I've been coming home so late."

"Mama already told me; it's because of overtime, right?"

"No, it's because I met a girl. Her name is Catalina." Mateo sheds a tear. "This wouldn't have happened—"

"Let me stop you right there," Oración says, interrupting her son. "Never blame this on anyone except those men." She tosses him the keys to his father's car. "Now go to her."

Mateo smiles and limps quickly to the car. The car is a well-groomed station wagon that has been under a tarp for years. It turns over without any issue, as his mother stated. With no time to waste, he drives to Catalina's house a few minutes away. When he arrives, he looks upon a run-down home that looks to have been built from different houses. The yard consists of dirt and large boulders. He climbs out of his father's vehicle and limps to her old, beaten-up door. He knocks, and Catalina opens.

"What are you doing, Mateo? And what's wrong with your leg?" She is horrified by his presence.

Mateo scratches the back of his neck and hesitates. "Well, I got into some trouble, and … and you see, I can't stay here in Mexico anymore, and—"

"You want me to go with you?" Catalina finishes the rest of his sentence for him with excitement.

"Yes," Mateo responds.

Catalina glances behind her and sees that her father is passed out from drinking and her mother is nowhere to be seen, as usual. "Okay, *un* minute."

With much eagerness, she cracks the door, smiling at Mateo and the thought of freedom. Hearing all types of rummaging in the house, Mateo limps back to his car. Holding a packed suitcase, Catalina opens and shuts her house door and quickly makes her way to the car. She opens the passenger's door and enters. "When did you get a car?"

Before Mateo can answer, he sees Catalina's house door swing open with force. Her father steps out, yelling for her.

"Never mind!" Catalina says. "Let's get out of this hellhole."

Mateo puts the car in reverse and spits gravel at her father while leaving. Catalina sees Mateo's wounds. "So what happened to you?"

Mateo looks into Catalina's eyes and pauses to elaborate on the most recent events. "A new start."

CHAPTER 22

THE BROTHERS LOOK AT ONE another after the story is told. Their fists clench at their new understanding of the connection their grandfather had with Mikhael and the fact that they were never told.

"So where are the keys?" Alex asks, sounding upset.

Gilbert walks over to the kitchen and moves piles of garbage from the countertop to locate them. "Sorry about the mess. If I knew you guys were coming over, I would have cleaned up a little more." He unloops the key from a chain holding other keys. "Here you go." He hands over the key to Alex. "I'll walk you to the car." Gilbert has the brothers follow out the house.

The three stand in front of the car parked under an aluminum carport connected to the house. The car is an Impala that is a few years old but still looks to be in good shape. The night sky keeps it from showing all the dents and scratches. It could easily be estimated as a $7,000 car. With the money the brothers are giving to him, Gilbert is getting more than double.

Gilbert shakes the brothers' hands. "Well, the car is all yours. Gas tank is about full, and it runs as if it were just bought off the lot yesterday. It has a built-in GPS as well. I never had a problem with it, so it should take you wherever you need to go."

Alex twirls the keys into the palm of his hands. "Okay, let's go."

Ricky nods to his brother, eager to continue. They both wave to Gilbert as they are adjusting to the car. They keep their farewell brief, as always leaving as fast as possible. Their cousin moves slowly, still not fully awake, back inside his home. Alex turns the engine over and heads off to Flint, Michigan, to finally confront Mateo.

CHAPTER 23

THE NEXT DAY, THE SUN is shining down and Mateo is sitting outside in a rocking chair next to his garage. He's looking up to the sky, enjoying the sun's rays while pondering his mistakes. A car that he hasn't seen before pulls up. The windows are too tinted to recognize who is behind the wheel. Believing Mikhael is still unknown to his grandsons, he figures the car must be a friend or relative. The fragile old man moves out of his rocking chair and casually makes his way to the Impala. He shields the sun from his eyes but still can't make out who is driving the car. His heart starts to pound now that he can slightly make out the passengers' tattoos, which seem to be gang related. Thoughts of Mikhael's men coming to kill him overwhelm his body as the window begins to roll down.

"Hey old guy, check out our new car!" Ricky yells out.

Mateo, registering his grandsons, lets out a sigh of relief. "So did you save my daughter from those monsters that took her?"

"Get in; we can talk about it as I show you how smooth this thing can run," Ricky responds.

Ricky gets out to let their grandfather sit in the passenger's seat out of respect.

Mateo looks back to the house, wondering whether he should tell his wife. The anticipation gets to him, and he decides to ride along without revealing his whereabouts to Catalina. "So, the girls, how are they?"

Alex ignores the question. "We bought this car from Cuz Gilbert." The car reverses and drives away from the home.

"He told us the real story of how you and Grandma came to the US and why you have a twitch in your neck," Ricky states, ignoring his grandfather's question as well.

Just as the brothers predicted, his face becomes bloodshot and his fingers start to twitch with nervousness. He remains silent.

Mateo studies Alex's actions as he turns off the main road and down a dirt road surrounded by a wooded area. For several minutes as they drive down the dirt road, not a single word is uttered. Only the nose of the engine is heard.

Mateo breaks the silence, worried about what his grandson's next actions might be. "So where we going?"

Alex finally speaks as they come closer to their destination. "On the drive here, we called everyone in the family and told them what you did," he tells his grandfather.

"They all want you gone." Ricky's eyes start to water as the car comes to a halt.

They become stationary in an empty area off the dirt road surrounded by tall grass. A deep hole has been dug there; a shovel remains stuck in a mound of soil. A pond lies beyond the trees and tall grass. They are miles away from civilization—so deep into the wilderness that not even the birds dare to reach this distance.

Fear strikes Mateo as he examines the hole. "So that's why no one has talked to me this morning?"

"This place was Ricky's idea. It's relaxing, right? A perfect place to rest without a bother." Alex wipes a tear from his eye as he speaks to his grandfather. He steps out of the car. "Get out." He pulls a small pistol from his waist, leaving the car moving toward Mateo's door.

Mateo's fear finally rises. "Please, mijos, you don't understand." His collar is grasped by Alex, who pulls the old man out.

"Shut up!" Rick waves his pistol at his grandfather as well. "How could you?" Ricky paces in a circle, frustrated, trying to calm his panicked state. "You know, when that piece of shit Mikhael told me it was your idea, I didn't want to believe him; but when Gilbert told me the true story of your neck, we figured it all out."

Alex drags his grandfather into the hole that they dug a few hours ago.

Ricky points his gun at Mateo, who is in a fetal position. "I had so much respect for you. How could you do this?" Tears start to fall down rapidly.

"Stop." Alex gently moves aside his brother's firearm, making sincere eye contact with him. "You have more respect for him than I do."

Mateo climbs to his knees. "Please, they said they will kill us all if not—"

Alex aims his weapon at Mateo to quiet him. "I'm truly sorry, Grandpa; it has to be like this." Alex closes his eyes and breathes in and out slowly to prepare himself. The world stops, and Mateo hears nothing. As Alex slowly squeezes the trigger, images of his grandfather being so kind to him as a child are playing in his head. "Ahh!" Alex yells with fury in his voice, battling his thoughts while playing tug-of-war with the trigger.

Moments later, the brothers find themselves back on the road, their tears from the intense battle with their emotions drying on their cheeks. The brothers don't mutter a word the whole time they're in the car, driving to the police station. Alex is ready to make his last move—turning himself in.

"Here's good," Alex tells his brother. "I don't want you to be an accessory, so a block away, out of the line of sight, will be fine."

Ricky pulls the car to the side of the road, wishing his brother good luck. "I love you, bro."

"I love you too." Alex exits the car and faces his older brother. He leans inside, reaching for Ricky's grasping hand. They embrace each other by pulling their bodies inward toward the hand clasp. Alex stands up after the moment comes to an end, gathers a breath of fresh air, and takes the sight in. "It's a beautiful day," he says to himself, preparing for the inevitable. Taking his time, the worn-out marine drags his feet into the police station with his head held high, prepared for interrogation.

CHAPTER 24

A DOORKNOB TURNS. A HEAVY metal door opens. Two military police escort Alex to a chair in an empty interrogation room with nothing surrounding the chair but five high-ranking officers of the military. They sit in front of Alex behind a long wooden table. Alex identifies one of these officers as his commanding officer with Rojas—the one who helped Rojas obtain the Predators.

"You may be seated," one speaks.

Alex sits while the two MPs stand at attention and salute the five men. The two pivot to the exit and march out of the room.

The remaining five look at one another. "Shall we get started?" one of them says. They all nod toward the one who is seated at the far left side of the table. "Sate your name and rank."

Alex situates his seating posture to be upright. "Corporal Alex Hernandez. I have been trained to be part of a special operative called MARSOC."

"Do you understand why there is no jury here and just us in this room?"

"Yes." Alex eyes all the officers in front of him, starting with the one who asked the first question, and brings his gaze to the officers' table, not making eye contact so as to respect their rank. "When I joined, I signed a contract stating that we are no longer citizens and that if I ever broke the law, there would not be a trial but a sentence."

"Good." The first to speak faces the officer beside him. A gesture is made to let her know she can begin her series of questions now.

"Now, you have turned yourself in for crimes you have committed, such as treason and termism. Is this correct?"

"Yes ma'am." Alex continues to eye the table while keeping his head in proper form.

"And we are to believe, you, alone, were capable of causing all this destruction in Mexico?"

Alex shows no hesitation. "That's correct."

She looks over to the left, just as the one before her did, to let the next officer ask a question.

"Ahem." The officer leans forward. This action causes Alex to lose slight focus and make eye contact. "Why did you do it?"

Several exhausting minutes pass by. Alex finishes explaining the situation he had to go through. He explains the several occurrences as though he acted alone, not mentioning the others.

The officer interrogating Alex stops glaring into his eyes and sits back, satisfied by the response. "You state that your grandfather is the one who sent your mother and younger siblings to their own deaths because of his history?"

"That is correct sir," Alex answers.

The officer leafs through some paperwork. "This paper states you have an older brother. Where was your brother at the time you were committing these crimes?"

Still sitting upright, a hand on each knee, still persistent with his story, he replies, "Showing comfort to our family in Flint, Michigan."

The officer holds up a piece of paper that Alex can see through. Ricky's face is printed on it. "This record states your brother has enough background history to help you." He places the paper down. "It says he was under investigation for multiple gang attacks. Why wouldn't he use his resources to help you?"

Alex shows no signs of false information. "He did want to help me; he contacted me and was the one who told me my mother was taken. When I arrived in the United States, I told him I was the only one who was properly trained for the task at hand. After explaining myself, he understood and went to my grandmother's house, where all my family was, and he waited with them."

"I'm still not convinced you were alone." The officer gives Alex a mean grin.

"There was another," Alex says, "but his trial is after mine. Sergeant Rojas."

"Yes, of course. Sergeant Rojas, who is accused of tampering with satellites and intercepting the military of Mexico to destroy the surrounding threat that had 'only you' trapped inside a building in the city of Saltillo. You state that afterward, you quickly made your way to Mikhael Trevijano Morales and executed him."

Alex grinds his teeth at the thought of Mikhael, keeping his composure. "Correct."

The officer interlocks his fingers and relaxes his shoulders, "I have no more questions at this time." He turns to the next officer, hinting that he has finished and she can begin her questions.

She opens a folder that Alex assumes is filled with evidence and information on Alex. It resembles the other officer's folders. She takes a few seconds to skim through the paperwork. When finished looking through the paperwork, she shuts the folder and taps her finger on the table. "What you did in Mexico, I believe, was done for a noble cause and was very justified, but my opinion does not matter—not until the verdict is arrived at. What I am in charge of here is the crimes you committed in America: AWOL, theft, and only God knows how many more. But I'm only interested in the ones I can prove. Right now, it is only AWOL. Unless you are willing to tell us more?" She raises an eyebrow and leans forward.

Alex doesn't budge. "AWOL is the only crime I committed in the United States."

"Fine." She leans back. "So tell us how you were able to leave a ship in the middle of the ocean?"

"After a reconnaissance mission, I was told to go to the meeting room where our troop commander would discuss our next task. After the meeting, I made my way to a plane. Its destination was America. I used my training and stealth to crawl into a box that was going to a factory outside of a military base. From there I waited until a worker from the plant opened the box. I startled them so much I was able to find my way out without any alarm."

She places her hands on top of her head and looks up to the ceiling to think. Her eccentric personality shows slightly as she rocks the chair back and forth. "What was your transportation?"

"I found a bus station, and from the bus dropping me off at the border, I swiftly sneaked into Mexico and paid for a taxi service. After I was deep enough into Mexico, I knew crimes could be easily committed. I stole a car and used that car the rest of the time."

The officer taps her fingers on the table, trying to understand the situation more in depth. "Okay, okay, so you covered almost everything, but I have one more question. Your grandfather, he's been missing for a while now. Do you know anything about that? No, I worded that wrong. Um … did you kill your grandfather?"

"There is no evidence showing that I killed anyone or having anything to do with a disappearance," Alex responds.

"No, I guess not. Well, very well, I'm done." She leans to the last officer. "Your turn."

He turns his head to Alex, and with the deepest voice out of all in the room, he says, "Mexico demands a trial in their court. We considered this, but intel shows that you would have been praised as a hero since you took out an entire cartel organization." The officer looks directly into Alex's eyes. "Now that the organization has been dismantled, the remaining cartel will be absorbed by the surrounding gangs. Still, these members will stay loyal to Los Unos. They will find a way to retaliate, making you a marked target until all of the cartel members are no more or you are terminated. Were you prepared for this when you entered Mexico?"

"Yes, I was aware of this, and I would sacrifice myself over and over to try to save my family from harm no matter the consequences," Alex states.

"We can give you only so much protection. They have people everywhere, maybe even in this room. That is another reason we did not agree to a trial in Mexico—they would not have given protection like us."

A slight smirk appears on Alex's face. "Thank you for the generosity, but I would like them to come for me. Like you said, they will keep coming until they are all gone, and this would make things a lot easier for me."

"You're very confident in your abilities, and you should be; only a select few can be a part of MARSOC." The officer scans the other officers at the table and looks back to Alex. "So what should your punishment be?"

Alex clears his throat and takes a second before saying, "Justified."

"Understood." The officer jolts, standing to his feet, causing his hands to slam onto the table with a clap.

★★★

Months later, birds sing as the beautiful sun beams down upon Alex. He stands from sitting behind an outside bench in a lounge area for visitors. He is surrounded behind a fenced-in brig. He hears the patter of small feet running toward him. It's his sister Stefani, who greets Alex with a diving hug. "Hello, sister, how are you?" he asks.

"I'm getting better. Ricky's been taking care of us ever since … well, you know." Stefani stops smiling and sits down on the bench, losing color in her face from the thoughts of her most recent past events.

Alex rubs the top of her head. "It's okay, you don't have to talk about it. I'm sorry for asking that question."

Kayla and Ricky follow a few seconds behind Stefani. They both greet Alex with a tight squeeze.

Ricky inspects Alex with an up-and-down stare. "You look good, bro."

Kayla agrees. "Yeah, you've been hitting the weights."

"Kind of." Alex flexes his bicep with a laugh. He then flops his body next to Stefani. "Come sit down." Alex invites his family to the bench.

Ricky places himself next to Kayla. "Ben, James, and Travis are here too. The rest of the family would have come, but you know how they are—never want to be a part of anything and probably still upset about Old Guy and what he did."

"Yeah, whatever. But that's cool that they are here. I take it Travis doesn't have a grudge anymore about him missing out on his honeymoon."

"Nah, I think the money we took from ol' dude and gave to his wife and him made them pretty happy." Ricky sniggers. "I'm still kind of upset that you took the rap."

"You know why I had to." Alex shows slight annoyance at having to repeat himself.

"Yeah, but it's the oldest sibling who's supposed to look after the younger ones." Ricky has battled himself day in and day out, trying to overcome his pride. Ricky raises his hand to Alex's face, interrupting his brother. "And let me stop you from saying anything more, cuz I know what you goin' to say." He changes his voice to imitate Alex's. "Yeah, but we are only a year apart. Whatever, man." Ricky then changes the subject before he starts to get aggravated. "Well, Ben, James, and I started an anti-gang affiliation."

Stefani snaps out of the daze, joining the conversation. "Yeah, they go around and raise money for the poor and go to schools and stuff."

Alex chuckles at Stefani's info, imagining his brother as a friendly man. "Wow, really? What's it called?"

"The same as what they called themselves before." Kayla replies.

"Really?" Alex looks confused.

Ricky gives a maniacal laugh. "Yup, you know we had to keep it real. And if anyone wants to step up and try to stop us, they know we won't take any crap."

"In other words, so people won't think you're a pushover organization." Alex shakes his head with a chuckle. "But that's good that you don't do crazy stuff anymore."

Ricky agrees. "Yeah, I wanted our city like Mexico, but after all we've been through, never mind. I know what it's like to be on the other side."

"Not to change the subject, but how long are you going to be here?" Kayla asks.

"Well, thanks to someone on the inside of the group of five who sentenced me, I was only charged with Article Eighty-Six AWOL."

"Eighty-Six AWOL? What's that?" Stefani asks.

"A special kind of absent without official leave." Alex answers.

"Wow, that's all?" Kayla's jaw drops. "After everything you've done?"

Alex shrugs. "Yeah, the cause was noble and justified, so everyone turned a blind eye to everything, but I had to have a punishment."

Ricky raises his eyebrow. "So how long is your sentence? And have you heard anything about Rojas?"

"A year and a half for me." Alex crosses his arms with smugness, his face filled with pride. "But Rojas"—he drops his arms out of grief—"he told me he got five years."

"A year and a half? Wow!" Ricky lets out a chuckle. "Now I understand a little more why you took the rap. But that really sucks about Rojas. How's he doing?"

"He's here with me and doesn't have any hard feelings about the whole situation. He tells me he has no regrets and would be willing to do it again, if you believe that..."

"That's good to hear," Ricky replies.

Alex shifts his body to face Kayla. "Well, I haven't heard how you are doing, Kayla?" Alex asks.

"Well, I have night terrors, and Stefani and I have to take classes with some counselor. But I think I'm getting better. I'm not ready to go back to school yet, and I don't think Stefani is either." Kayla bows her head with sadness. "I miss Mom and Brittany a lot."

Alex takes a deep breath in. "Yeah, we all do."

Quietness strikes, but only for a brief moment. Ricky, being the clown of the siblings as always, thinks of a way to lighten the mood. He lets one rip, and the entire bench shakes. "That's a spicy meatball," he says aloud with an Italian accent.

"OMG! You're so gross." Kayla holds her nose closed.

Alex laughs and waves his hand near his nose. "Yup, pretty spicy."

"Wow, really," Stefani says with a blank facial expression, and then she proceeds to laugh hysterically.

They talk, laugh, and reminisce for another hour or so. Not wanting to take up all the visiting hours, they proceed to make their way to the exit to let Ben, James, and Travis come next. Alex walks them to the entrance they came in from. He gives his two sisters a hug and a kiss on their foreheads. He punches his brother in the arm to open a friendly tussle. The visit ends with a laugh.

As they sluggishly leave, but before the door shuts behind them, the girls turn their heads to make eye contact with Alex one more time. They smile from ear to ear to show Alex how sincere they both are. Their body language shows the gratitude they are expressing with much endearment.

Alex nods to acknowledge their message before softly moving back to the bench where they were sitting. He faces the open field beyond the fence with his chin resting on his interlocked fingers, waiting for the others.

"Alex!"

He hears his name spoken simultaneously with some slight laughter behind it. Travis, Ben, and James giggle among each other as if they are teenagers, rushing Alex. Alex shakes his head before turning around to see his friends engaging in their ridiculousness. He smiles at the thought of the joy his next conversations will bring.

Printed in the United States
by Baker & Taylor Publisher Services